GETTING DIRTY

GETTING DIRTY

A Jail Bait Novel

MIA STORM

Getting Dirty

Cover Design: Sarah Hansen, Okay Creations

To Katy,

for making me brave.

CHAPTER 1

Blaire

My nipples are hard, and the heat radiating off his body, only inches behind me, makes them harder.

My palms are slick, and no matter how often I wipe them on my baggy jeans, they don't dry.

My diaphragm is tight with anticipation, and I know he must be able to hear my shaky breath.

I am burning alive, even though I know they keep the library cool so exhausted students don't fall asleep and drool on their books.

When Professor Duncan sent me to the resource desk at the university library and told me to ask for his graduate assistant, Caiden Brenner, I had no idea. I've dated a few boys at school, and I've even had sex once, but I can't remember my body ever reacting this way to being near a guy—seizing up and refusing to participate in any semblance of normal behavior. Maybe that's because, no matter how hot they are, teenage boys smell rank.

"Is this it?" Caiden asks.

His firm chest presses against my shoulder as he leans over me to reach for a book on the second shelf, well above my head, and he most certainly does *not* smell rank. His cologne (or maybe it's just his deodorant) combined with some warm, earthy scent spins me in a cocoon of heady sensations I don't even have names for.

He brings the book down and backs away a step as he opens it. "*Don Juan* by Byron, right? This the one you were looking for?"

His tongue slips out for a moment as he scans the page, drawing my attention to full, firm lips that aren't quite symmetrical. Both upper and lower are just a little fuller on the left. But they're wet now, and the fluorescents overhead shine off creases and curves the exact color of the coral sheets on the double bed I left unmade this morning.

The thought conjures the image of Caiden twisted into those sheets and not only do my nipples tighten more, but a hot ache starts low in my belly.

As his eyes scan the first few pages, I take the opportunity to burn his image into my retinas for later. There's a faint star-shaped scar on the right side of a nose that's on the small side and flares out at the bottom. My gaze trails along his thick, curved, golden eyebrows, across a broad, smooth forehead with a flat, dark mole near the hairline on the left, and down the curl of longish honey brown hair that hangs over his right eye—an eye that is blue, but just barely. Under the blue of his irises is something darker, like steel gray storm clouds gathering behind a twilight sky.

They lift to mine and I look away quickly. Then I realize it's a little too obvious that I'm trying to *not* look at him, so I lift my gaze from his black Vans to the book in his hands.

His hands.

They're long, with smooth, bronze skin and clean, trimmed fingernails. I don't know why I'm noticing his fingernails, except every little thing about him fascinates me.

I tear my eyes away from his hands, and when I can't think of a single normal thing to do with them except look at his face again, I find him staring at me with an amused expression—just a slight uptick of the fuller side of his mouth and a glint in his gaze.

With a jolt, I remember he asked me something. He's waiting for an answer. My cheeks warm as I wrack my brain, replaying the last few seconds.

The *book*. He asked if it was the right book.

"Yeah, thanks," is all I can manage through the haze of lust hanging over me like the clouds in his eyes.

He looks back down at the book and flips a page. "I used to be a fan of Lord Byron's work, but lately I've discovered just how tedious he can be. He's incredibly self-indulgent." He lifts the book slightly. "You realize this one poem is sixteen hundred lines? That's six thousand more than Milton's *Paradise Lost*, and that one's epic. This one's just ridiculous." He snaps the book shut. "If I had to pick which nineteenth century poet to hang out with, it would be William Blake, hands down. People called him warped, or worse, but nothing he wrote is boring, that's for damn sure."

I barely hear what he's saying, because watching his lips move is absorbing all of my attention.

I'm not usually a dribbling idiot. I can't even define the reason this man has suddenly turned me into one. But I can't deny he has.

Honestly, I'm really interested in the Romantic movement and how poetry evolved from that into what we're writing now. I was seriously excited when I got instructor permission to register for an upper level poetry class just for that reason. This is the kind of conversation I'm starving for and could *never* find in high school, even with my English teachers. The things he's saying should be captivating me, but I find what's captivating me instead is his slightly lopsided mouth and his storming eyes and his expressive hands that move as he talks.

This is my second semester taking evening classes at Sierra State University. Mrs. Erikson, my Junior Honors English teacher at Oak Crest High suggested it because our little school, tucked into the foothills, is too small to offer many AP classes. I'm enrolled in AP calculus and history, but we don't have AP English.

"Most students applying to Stanford and UC Berkeley will have well over a 4.0 GPA, with the AP bump they'll get from courses at their high schools," she'd said when she called me before the start of my senior year to express her concern. "It will help that you're valedictorian, but if you truly hope to be admitted as a literature major, you'll need to show them you've excelled in college level English via some other avenue."

Last semester I took written composition, or basic freshman English, and Professor Duncan's assignments didn't stray from the class reading too much, so I never set foot in the library. I aced it, and when he found out I write poetry, he suggested his upper level Early Nineteenth Century Poetry class for this semester. He assured me I could handle it and signed off on the prerequisite waiver.

So here I am, researching Byron for a presentation at the end of the semester.

"All right, then..." Caiden says, and I realize, once again, he's been waiting for some kind of reply from me. He hands me the book. "Good luck with your project."

"I'm supposed to analyze Don Juan's sexual conflict," I blurt, taking the book from him. My face goes instantly hot and I hate the blood that betrays me by rising to my cheeks.

The amusement is back in his eyes. "Byron definitely takes a different approach to the classic Don Juan legend." He starts toward the resource desk and I follow at his side. "Most interpretations, including Molina, Espronceda, and even Mozart, portray him as a womanizing libertine without any moral compass. Byron flips that stereotype on its head, presenting him as a young, conflicted casualty of nonexistent self-restraint when it comes to feminine temptations—more the victim than the aggressor."

Caiden's profile is perfect. This is what I'm thinking when it occurs to me I should say something. "So it's the girls' faults he sleeps around?"

The hint of a smile ticks the left side of his mouth as he ducks his head slightly. A rush prickles at the base of my spine then spreads when I realize I've embarrassed him. And now my nipples are even harder.

His eyes flick to me as we reach the desk and he moves behind it. "According to Byron, yes."

I lay the book on the counter, shifting a hip up to join it. "Which version do you like better?"

He reaches for the book, and I catch the sweep of his eyes over my body before they lower back to the scanner and he scans the barcode. With the action, I'm mentally kicking myself for wearing my frumpiest sweater. I just never thought...

"It's said that Mozart based his Don Juan on Casanova, who was in attendance at the first performance of Mozart's opera. If you believe the stories, there are men like Casanova out there." He lifts his eyes but not his head, looking at me out from under long golden lashes. "But I think most men are more like Byron's version—sort of helpless when it comes to resisting a beautiful woman."

The rush to my groin is sudden and intense.

I've felt this rush before. At the beginning of the school year, when I saw the guys in my class notice that I finally filled out over the summer, there was an undeniable tingle in my groin. I liked the feeling of being checked out. There was something empowering about knowing, just for that second, I had a boy's complete attention. But when the tingling passed a second later, that was it. I'd never felt the hot pulsing ache between my legs that I feel right now—swollen and wet and wanting.

He holds the book out to me. "This is due back on January twenty ninth; two weeks. If you need it after that, I should be able to renew it unless one of your classmates has requested it."

I make sure my fingers brush his as I take it. "Thanks."

I feel his eyes on me as I walk toward the stairs and sway my hips just a little more than usual. Though, in my loose jeans, the effect is probably lost. I turn back at the landing and see him watching after me. I lift a hand before turning the corner.

He's Professor Duncan's graduate assistant. How old would that make him? He's no boy, that's for damn sure. The stubble on his chin was very short and even, as if he'd gone maybe a day without shaving. Two at the most. Very few of the boys in my class could pull that off. When they decide not to shave during football season or whatever, their beards are mangy-looking with bald patches.

If he's a graduate student, he has to be at least twenty-two. Probably older. I'm sure I was just imagining that he seemed into me. Wishful thinking. What would he want with a high school girl?

But then it occurs to me he wouldn't know.

And I plan to keep it that way.

"How was class, honey?" Mom asks when I come through the door. She doesn't look up from her crossword.

And Dad doesn't wake from where he's snoring in the recliner.

I toss my messenger bag to the floor near the stairs and slip the empty highball glass out of his hand, where it's precariously balanced on the arm of the chair, wedged into the webbed space between his thumb and index finger. He snorts and his foot jerks on the leg rest, but he doesn't wake.

He's a harmless drunk. He buries himself in his job all day, and I guess he's really good at it, but as soon as he's home, he's got a drink in his hand. I think it's his escape. Work is easy for him, calculations and formulas and very little human interaction. Dealing with his family is an entirely different story. We're messy, unpredictable, and human, and don't fit into any algorithm or formula. I've never had an actual conversation with my father. He's more like an acquaintance from the neighborhood—the guy you have an awkward exchange about the weather with when you cross paths putting the garbage out or picking up the mail from the box.

"This one's going to be a lot more work than last semester," I say, crossing to the kitchen and putting Dad's glass on the counter. I tug open the fridge and grab a can of Diet Coke, making a mental note of what we need. I can stop at the store on my way home from school tomorrow, since I only have night class on Mondays, Wednesdays, and Fridays.

She erases something on her puzzle. "You need to update your Stanford application and be sure they know you're taking a five hundred level literature class."

"And Berkeley," I add.

"And Berkeley," she repeats absently, adjusting her glasses and scowling at her puzzle. She went to Stanford, so I think she forgets there are other options.

I only seriously applied to Stanford and UC Berkeley. UC Davis is my fallback, but my high school guidance counselor is pretty sure it won't come to that. Berkeley's Literature program is more rooted in the classics, so it's my first choice.

Mom jots something down, then immediately erases it. "Marcus is heading back to school Sunday morning. You should plan to be here for dinner tomorrow night to say goodbye."

"Surprised he didn't have to be back sooner for training," I say, popping the tab on my Coke.

"Guess his coach decided they've earned winter break off after winning that tournament last month."

My brother and I could be the same person...if I was two years older and a six foot four guy. We look just alike, with Dad's wavy espresso hair, Mom's amber eyes, and skin that doesn't tan no matter how much time we spend in the sun—which is a lot, considering we both play water polo. Marcus graduated valedictorian of his class last year, but his focus was always more on athletics. He's on a full-ride water polo scholarship at UCLA, which he chose because they consistently rank at the top of their conference. "That tournament" they won last month was the NCAA Championship. It was a huge deal, televised and everything. But I don't think Mom really gets it.

The brains, Marcus and I can't really take too much credit for. Mom is a biochemical engineer and Dad is a nuclear physicist. They both have multiple degrees, Mom's from Brown and Stanford, and Dad's from Harvard and Cornell. They met at Platinum Biomedical, where they both work. Which makes sense, because in addition to the fact they're both cripplingly socially awkward, work is all either of them ever do. They're out the door at the crack of dawn, before I'm even up for school, and never home before eight or nine at night. From the time we were six weeks old, Marcus and I were raised by the nice ladies at Marie's House of Discovery and Day Care Center.

Marie had been a kindergarten teacher for nine years before she became unbearably frustrated with the "one size fits all" approach to teaching in public schools. She quit so she could open a learning center and do her own thing. And because she was a total '60s hippy throwback, her own thing involved a lot of self-discovery. (Thus, the House of *Discovery*.) From the time we were old enough to talk, we sat in circles and discussed our feelings every morning. Where public schools suspended kids for touching each other, at Marie's it was encouraged. (I'm pretty sure Marcus got his first hand job from Uma Newman before we aged out of the after school program at the end of fifth grade.) But where Marie's true gift lay was in discovering each kid's strengths and playing to them. Where Marcus's and my IQs might have been a gift from our parents, Marie is the one who nurtured those synapses to form and multiply. She made learning exciting.

After fifth grade, Marcus and I took care of each other. I don't think either of us were ever really aware of what triggered our drive to overachieve, but we fed off each other. Pushed each other. When we were little, it might have been our parents' attention we craved, but as we got older, we found out each other's was enough.

"Where is he?" I ask, just now realizing Marcus's car was gone from the curb when I came in.

"Out with Nathan. I think he's staying over there." Her brow creases. "Or maybe Nate's staying here. Don't remember what he said."

My stomach does a somersault. I've managed to avoid Nate the entire winter break. He and Marcus have been out partying for most of it, but I'm still surprised

I've made it this far without stumbling into him in the bathroom or whatever. But there's no way I can avoid him for the rest of my life. Since Marcus and Nate were in elementary school, Nate's spent more time here than at his own house. The three of us have always been tight. I don't want to screw that up because he's weird about fucking me. If he's here tonight, I'll talk to him. We need to clear the air, or else things will only get weirder.

"I'm heading up," I say, grabbing my Coke and slinging my bag over my shoulder. "I've got a ton of homework."

"'Night, honey," she says without looking up from her puzzle.

This is how it's always been in my house. Just going through the motions. Mom's obligated to love me and Marcus. Dad's just calling it in.

When I get to my room, I spend a few hours working through my calculus and history homework, then read the recently published part four of *Jonathan Livingston Seagull* for senior English. My teacher, Mr. Bates is an existentialist and the head of our local Transcendental Meditation Society chapter. I wasn't too sure about his reading list at first, but now I'm interested in checking out more of Richard Bach's work. After a quick Google search, I decide to ask Mr. Bates about *The Bridge Across Forever* tomorrow, then pull *Don Juan* from my bag and crack it open.

At the stroke of midnight, same as every other night, the TV clicks off downstairs and Mom wakes Dad and shuffles him across the family room to their bedroom next to the kitchen. It's an hour later when my eyelids get heavy and the words on the page stop making sense. I pull myself up and head to the bathroom to get ready for bed. I'm just padding back to my room when I hear Marcus and Nate slam through the front door, laughing and wrestling, based on the sound of things crashing downstairs.

Heavy bodies start smashing and banging up the stairs, a slurry of insults like "suck my fat cock" and "bite me" coming from the melee. My brother and his best friend slam into the wall on the landing with a loud thud that shakes the floor under my feet. Nate has Marcus in a headlock, but Marcus has Nate's knee cinched over his shoulder. I can't believe they're making any progress up the stairs at all. What progress they are making is slow, so I have plenty of time to duck into my room before they see me. But I don't. I wait near my door as they fight their way to the top.

"There she is!" my brother yells, letting go of Nate and lowering his shoulder as he charges toward me. I don't even have time to get out of the way before he takes my feet right out from under me and has me hiked over his shoulder with my ass in the air. I can smell the stale cigarettes on his T-shirt as I hang over his back. I'm sure he wasn't smoking, but Nate probably was. As were a lot of other people at whatever party they were at.

"Put me down!" I shout, pounding his back with my fists. Marcus is six four, and it feels like I'm about a mile off the ground.

"Whatever you say, sis." Marcus slides me off his shoulder and sets me back on my feet.

I turn and Nate is grinning at me from the top of the stairs, his deep dimples turned up full blast. He's closer to my five nine with a solid wrestler's body, and he likes his T-shirts tight to show off his defined arms and chest, the V of his back, and some drool-worthy abs. He probably weighs more than Marcus even though he's half a foot shorter.

I'd crushed on Nate for most of my freshman and sophomore years, while he and Marcus were a year ahead of me, tearing up our high school and taking no prisoners. He could date anyone he wanted, whenever he wanted. And that was never me.

Even though I hated it, I knew why he never thought of me as anything but Marcus's little sister. I *looked* like Marcus's little sister. But for my sixteenth birthday in May, someone must have mail ordered me boobs. I went from an A cup to a C overnight, and by August, though my size five jeans still fit, they were very snug through the hips and thighs.

The night before he and Marcus left for college, Nate finally noticed me, and though I'd never been with anyone else, I let him notice *all* of me. I don't regret it. If I was going to cash in my V-card, he seemed like a better choice than any of the other guys I knew from school. I trusted him, so I wasn't scared. He knew it was my first time and he went slow. It wasn't great, but it wasn't awful either. It felt really good to be the sole focus of his attention for that half hour. The fact that he didn't call before he left for school didn't surprise me. I never really expected anything more from him.

But I'm pretty sure Marcus doesn't know. Things wouldn't be this easy between them now if he knew his best friend had stolen his little sister's virtue five months ago.

Nate's charcoal eyes flash and instantly I know where his mind is. The same place as mine. But I also know he won't give us away by saying anything inappropriate in front of Marcus.

He walks over to me and holds out his arms. "Give papa some sugar."

Okay...except that. But he's always said that, even before he fucked me.

I step into his arms and his hug is a little tighter and a lot longer than usual. "Missed you, baby girl."

"How's Nevada?" I ask when he lets me go.

"Cold as a witch's tit." His eyes are still alight and they warm me from the inside out. "Marcus says you applied to Stanford. That's like..." He trails off and makes the "mind blown" gesture with his hands next to his ears. "You have any fucking clue how hot a girl with brains is?"

Marcus punches his arm and throws him a dirty look. "Stop fucking hitting on my little sister, dude!"

Nate's eyebrows go up and he fists his hand into his longish dark hair. "Have you *seen* your little sister? She's hot."

Okay…so maybe I was giving Nate too much credit.

"You lay a finger on her and I break it off and shove it up your ass," Marcus threatens.

I take that as my cue. "I'm gonna hit the sack," I say, gesturing toward my door with a wave of my hand. "But it was great to see you, Nate."

He pulls me into another hug. "Yeah, baby girl. You too. I been missing on you."

I slip through the door just as Marcus takes Nate to the floor. I hear them bash against walls as they migrate farther down the hall to Marcus's room, and then they're pounding against his furniture and the wall between our rooms.

I catch myself smiling as I climb under the covers. He missed me. I don't want to read anything into that, but I can't help wondering if I left a bigger impression on him than I thought. I drift off to the familiar sounds of the two boys I grew up with and realize just as I slip into sleep how much I miss them when they're gone. The house is lonelier without them.

Rain has started during the night. I wake to the soft beating of fat drops on the roof and window. I also wake to warm breath in my face and a hot, thick body in the bed next to me.

"Hey, baby girl," Nate breathes, his wet lips caressing my cheek as they move.

My heart starts to race as I roll to face him. "Hey. I'm guessing Marcus doesn't know you're here."

He shakes his head, the tip of his nose rubbing against mine. "Had to wait till he passed out."

I reach for his face and brush my fingers down his cheek. There's stubble that feels like silk when I brush down, and needles when I brush up. He's grown up this year too.

His lips seal over mine and I kiss him back. He tastes a little like sour beer, but I don't let that stop me. I've always loved Nate, and though most of that time it's been more of a brotherly sort of love, I really like the feeling of his body in this bed with me. I really like the feeling of his mouth, growing hungrier on mine.

I open my mouth for him and his tongue invades me, wrestling with mine the way he wrestled with my brother earlier, putting every ounce of himself into it.

I reach for his boxers and push them lower, then I nurture his hard-on, feel it grow with the love I'm giving him with my mouth and hands and body.

He lifts my T-shirt and tugs my panties down, and I kick them off. His fingers slip inside me and he moans a little in my ear, then kisses me harder as he fingers me.

I rock my hips with the motion of his hand and stroke his dick. I feel it swell tighter as he takes his mouth off mine and sucks in a breath.

"Do you have a condom?" I ask, because I might want sex with Nate, but I'm not so crazed that I don't remember the logistics of the birds and the bees.

He rolls to the side and feels for something on the floor, then lays me on my back and kneels between my legs. I hear the tear of paper. The muscles in my groin contract as I wait for him to fix it in place, knowing what comes next.

His weight presses down on me and I spread my legs. And then I feel him pressing inside me.

The first time we did this—the only other time I've done this—he had to push pretty hard to get inside and it stung a little, but I didn't bleed or anything. This time, there's no sting. He guides himself in with his hand, then starts to move, pumping against me. His breathing becomes more ragged, little groans escaping on puffs of air. He feels good inside me and I do my best to move with him. After a little while he stops moving and holds his breath.

"You feel so fucking good," he says when he lets it out. "I don't want to come yet." He starts pumping again. "Are you feeling me, baby girl?"

"Yeah," I say, because I am.

I feel heat from the friction of his skin rubbing against mine, and his hair brushing my cheek. I feel his mouth on mine and when he pulls away to breathe, I feel his hot breath on my lips. I feel full of him and happy he came to me. Happy that he wants me.

And when he thrusts hard into me one last time and groans, "Oh fucking Christ," I feel powerful. I like that I can make him feel something that intense. I love that I can make him lose control, if only for a second.

He lays on top of me for a few more minutes, catching his breath. "I've missed you so fucking much," he breathes into my hair. "Nobody else feels like you, baby girl."

It's okay if it's a lie. I'm not jealous of the other girls he's been with. There's no point to that. "Missed you too, Nate."

He pulls out of me and lays on his side facing me. "You know how fucked up this is, right? Me wanting my best friend's baby sister."

I shrug. "I'm not really a baby anymore."

"Fuck, no," he says, brushing his fingers over my nipple through my T-shirt. He kisses the tip of my nose then sits up and peels off his condom. He rakes his boxers off the floor and pulls them up his legs as he staggers toward the door.

I know this is what it is and I've always been okay with that. I don't expect any sort of commitment or anything long term from Nate. But I watch as he vanishes into the hall and can't help but wonder how long it will be before I hear from him again.

CHAPTER 2

Caiden

I know my interest in this girl is beyond inappropriate. I work for the university. I'm a few months from finishing my PhD in Comparative Literature. At twenty-five, unless she were a senior, she's way too young to be on my radar. But there's something about her I find mesmerizing.

I desperately want to ask her how old she is, but even just the question hints at impropriety. She's in Dr. Duncan's upper level poetry class, so she's probably at least a junior, though he takes an occasional sophomore. So...twenty-ish?

Too young, I remind myself.

When she first came in last week, dressed in a loose sweater and low-slung jeans, it was easy to overlook the fact that she has some very nice curves.

But not today.

Against my will, my eyes track her to a table near the back of the resource center. I try to ignore my body's reaction as I take in the full measure of toned leg between the heeled boots and her short skirt. I seriously doubt she gained the traditional freshman fifteen. Everything about her looks flat and firm under her snug-fitting sweater.

My body *can't* have a reaction to her. Messing with the undergrads in Dr. Duncan's class would get me booted out of here faster than you could say Don Juan.

She slips into a seat and glances my direction. I duck my head, pretending I wasn't just totally checking her out. I busy myself behind the counter cataloging new references that Dr. Duncan has added to his reading list this semester. But there's no way cataloging can hold my attention when she's only thirty feet away.

I'm forcing my eyes back to my work just as a loud, "Fucking—umph!" comes from the direction of the stairs.

I spin in time to catch Jones, fellow grad school compatriot and my kickboxing partner, demonstrate perfect belly flop technique as he sprawls face down at the top of the stairs. His messenger bag first flips up and clubs him in the head, then flies open and spews its contents across ten feet of floor in a veritable yard sale.

I'm thinking I should go over there and help him when, in my peripheral vision, I see Blaire crossing toward the stairs. I'm out from behind the counter like a shot.

I chose Jones as my kickboxing partner because I needed someone who could push me. He's six three, two inches taller than me, and outweighs my two ten by a solid twenty pounds. He's got that rough around the edges thing going that ladies seem to dig on. And, unlike me, he's an unrestricted free agent. His grandmother is footing his grad school bills, so he hasn't had to grovel for scholarships, graduate assistantships, and work-study gigs to pay tuition. Meaning, he can date anyone he wants. And he does. He doesn't have any qualms about dipping into the undergrad dating pool.

I get to him a hair ahead of Blaire and haul him up by an arm.

"Every. Fucking. Time," he mutters with a scowl over his shoulder at the offending stair. "I'm going to sue the hell spawn who built that last stair deeper than the others."

"Are you okay?" Blaire asks, kneeling down and brushing up some papers fanning from a yellow folder that fell out of his bag.

He's momentarily dumbstruck, and that's before his eyes even turn to her. It's her voice—silk over sandpaper. Rough with just a little bit of purr on the kick. Super sexy. And when his eyes find her, I swear he fucking drools.

I shove one of his books in his chest to snap him out of it.

"That's my usual entrance," he says, putting on a cocky smirk and flicking his wrist at the stairs. "What did you think?"

She hands him the file and another book she's scooped up and smiles. "You're a great flier, but your landing could use some work."

He takes his things from her and tucks them into his bag, grinning like a moron. "I've never been quite able to stick it."

She shrugs. "Sorry. The best I can give you is a seven point two."

I see his expression shift and know he's getting ready to swoop in for the kill.

"Was there something you needed, Jones?" I say, turning for the desk, hoping he'll follow. But even if he doesn't, I can't stand here and bear witness to him hitting on Blaire.

"Yeah." He thankfully follows and when I get to the desk and turn back, I see Blaire heading to her table. And Jones's eyes glued to her ass. "Do you know who that is?" he asks, his voice lower.

I shake my head. "All I know is she's in Duncan's poetry class."

He nods slowly and doesn't say anything else.

"I'm sure you came here for a reason other than to ogle the undergrads."

Finally, his eyes shift to me. "Just needed that Hemingway biography."

I bring him around the side of the stacks farthest from Blaire and find his book, but when I hand it to him, he's peering through the shelves to where we can just catch a glimpse of her. I shove the book at him. "Stop being a fucking pervert."

"She's hot," he says with a small shake of his head, "and I don't think she's wearing a bra."

I shove him toward the stairs. "Like I said, stop being a fucking pervert."

When we round the corner near the tables, he raises his voice and says, "So, I'll be kicking your ass again in the ring on Monday, yes?"

I laugh under my breath and mutter, "Yeah. Good luck with that."

Jones might be bigger than me, but I'm quicker. It's usually a pretty even match.

"We'll see if you're still laughing while I'm pounding you into the mat."

His voice is still too loud, and when I look up, I see it's had the desired effect. Blaire is watching us.

I shove him toward the stairs. "Whatever."

"I'll work on that landing," he says with a wave her direction.

She smiles, and when he shifts like he's going to head her way, I thump a palm into his chest.

His attention snaps to me. "You cock blocking me, man?" he mutters.

I cut him a look.

Understanding dawns on his face and his eyes widen. "You thinking about tapping that?"

I shake my head. "Get the fuck out of my library."

He grins and turns for the stairs. "Didn't think you had it in you," he calls over his shoulder.

When he's finally gone I return to the desk and focus on the cataloging. As long as I keep my eyes down and my back turned, I can almost pretend the sexiest woman I've ever laid eyes on isn't just thirty feet away.

"Excuse me."

So much for thirty feet. My insides seize and heart slams against my ribcage at the sound of her voice just behind me. When I turn, she's standing on the other side of the counter, leaning forward on her hands. Her sable hair lays in loose waves to nearly her waist, contrasting with skin the color of cream. Her shimmering whiskey-colored eyes search mine for something and I'm dying to ask her what. The way she's looking at me, I'd give her anything. Her arms push her breasts up and in, and her nipples bead tightly against the fabric of her heather gray sweater. And Jones was right. She's not wearing a bra.

My dick stiffens before I can will it into submission.

"Blaire, right?" I say, stepping toward the counter.

She smiles, her plump cherry lips puckering just so. "Right. Didn't think you'd remember."

There's no fucking way I'd forget. "Not too many Blaires around here. You made an impression," I say, smiling back.

Am I fucking flirting with her? Christ, I've got to rein myself in.

"Thanks for helping Jones," I add quickly with a gesture at the stairs.

"That was quite the entrance." The hint of a wily smile quirks her lips and a stone sinks in my gut with the fleeting thought that she's about to ask me for his number. "But, now *I* could use *your* help." She props a hip on the counter and leans back on her hand.

I force my gaze off her chest and glue it to her stunning eyes, the color of well-aged scotch. "What is it you needed?"

"I read through the first five cantos of *Don Juan* and I was hoping to bounce some thoughts off you, since you seem to have an opinion on the whole thing."

I give her a slow nod. "Let me just finish up a few things here, then I'm all yours."

"I'll be over there," she says, pointing to her things on the table, as if I wasn't already painfully aware of exactly where she was.

"I'll be right over."

I don't mean to watch her go, but that's where my eyes are until she lowers herself back onto her chair. I turn and adjust my jeans around my stiff cock, then go back to cataloging until it's under control. I look at her a long moment, her back to me, testing myself. Once I've determined that my cock is, in fact, under my control, not hers, I step around the counter and slide into the seat across from her so I can keep an eye on the desk.

"So, what were your thoughts on the first five cantos?" I ask, tapping her open copy of *Don Juan* with my finger.

She leans back in her chair and watches my hand. "Is it just me, or is Don Juan a horribly flat character?"

"You've discovered what I was saying about Byron being self-indulgent. Juan is often more a plot device than a character. The narrator is subsumed into Byron himself much of the time. As you move deeper into the poem, you'll find Byron becomes more central to the poem than Juan."

"So he wrote about himself?"

I pull the book closer and flip to Canto III. "You read this, right?" I ask, turning it for her to see.

Her expression turns incredulous. "Yeah. What the hell was that, anyway? Byron totally hijacked the poem and started dissing on Coleridge, Wordsworth and…some other guy."

I nod. "Robert Southey. And then there's the whole section at the end with a different verse in which Byron gives us his opinion on the fact that Greece is under Ottoman control."

"Which has nothing to do with Juan or anything else," she finishes.

"But has everything to do with Byron," I say, flipping to the end of the book. "He died from injuries he received at war fighting for Greece's independence while he was in the middle of writing Canto seventeen. The adventures of Don Juan themselves are thought, in certain literary circles, to be poetic re-imaginings of Byron's own escapades and dysfunctional relationships with the women in his life. Basically an imaginative autobiography wherein Byron retells the classic story of Don Juan with himself as the womanizer." I lean back. "Like writing himself into his own porn."

When she smiles and lowers her lashes, I realize I said what I just did to see what her reaction would be. I need to rein myself back. She's totally off-limits.

"But why would he want to portray himself like that," she says, lifting her eyes back to mine. "I mean, Don Juan's kind of an idiot. I get that he's sixteen and all, but it seems like he's just sort of stumbling around here and there and lands dick first in women's crotches totally by accident."

And, *Christ*. She just picked up my innuendo and dished it right back.

Game fucking on.

I lean forward onto my elbows. "That's true in a lot of ways. As I said, he's generally the pursued in Byron's version."

Her eyes scan down my face to my chest, then over my biceps. It's only with her scrutiny that I realize how tightly I'm clenching every muscle in my body, trying to keep it from responding to her presence.

"And he seems to like it," she says, her eyes lifting back to mine.

I swallow when I feel my dick twitch to life again. "Yes. But what sixteen-year-old boy wouldn't."

"But his lovers are all older." Her gaze twitches to my left hand, where it lays on her open copy of *Don Juan*, then back to my eyes. "And married."

"And, therein lies his conflict."

"He doesn't really seem that conflicted." She leans closer and lowers her voice. "He just fucks them."

Fuck. There's nothing I can do to stop my hard-on from raging. "Keep reading. Things go downhill fast." Because they always do when you fuck people you're not supposed to.

She leans back and pulls the book out from under my hand. "You'll work it through with me? Because, I've got to tell you, I'm not seeing the conflict."

"What year are you?" I don't even realize I've said it until it's out of my mouth.

Her eyes flick from the book to mine. "A senior."

I feel my eyebrows arch before I can stop them. "You look younger."

She bites her lips between her teeth for a moment. "Is that good or bad?"

"Neither, I suppose." But my insides burn, knowing that she's not as off-limits as I originally thought. It's nearing the end of January. Commencement will be here soon enough. She graduates and all bets are off.

"So..." she says, twisting a finger into the ends of her hair. "I know you like old, dead poets. How do you feel about hearing something fresher?"

I lean toward her. "Such as?"

"I'm reading in a poetry slam tonight. It's just something over at Tino's in Jonestown on the fourth Friday of every month. There's no prize money or anything, but I perform something new pretty much every month."

"A poetry slam..." I want to say yes in the worst way, but it feels dangerously like a date.

She must read the hesitation in my eyes. "If it's too weird, no worries. I just thought, since you like poetry…"

She leaves the thought dangling. Like a noose. And I jump right into it. "Yeah. Why not?"

The answer to that rhetorical question is that it's not May yet and she hasn't graduated. I'm risking everything I've worked the last three years toward. My entire future. But the voice of reason is being drowned out by the raging waves of something rolling up from the deepest layers of my being like an undertow. Something base and essential. And unrelenting.

"Do you want to meet me there?" she asks, standing from her seat and giving me a better view of the entire exquisite length of her.

"Yeah…that's probably best." Plausible deniability. *No, Dr. Duncan, I didn't have any clue she'd be there. Just went to hear the poetry.*

"Great," she says as she gathers her book and shoves it in her bag. "It starts at nine. There are usually five or six poets and it's a random draw, so I don't know what time I'll be reading."

I nod without standing, no longer able to tame my erection. "I'll be there at nine."

"You know where Tino's is?"

Electricity crackles under my skin. I'm really doing this. "Yeah. I'll find it."

I feel better about the whole thing when I walk into Tino's. The bar is very dimly lit except for the spotlight on the MC up on the stage. He's a blond kid, probably twenty, with a top hat and a flair for the dramatic. As I move deeper into the room and my eyes adjust, I don't see anyone I know. Including Blaire.

I find a seat at an empty table for two tucked into the back corner near the bar, and a toothpick thin waitress comes over for my drink order.

"What's your house scotch?" I ask, needing something stiffer than a beer to calm my jitters.

"Johnny Walker Red," she says, jutting a bony hip and fisting her hand on it. "Want some?"

"Sounds good. Make it a double."

"You got it," she says, already twitching toward the bar.

Onstage, the MC finishes announcing the first poet, and an Asian woman takes the stage. I lean back in my seat and rub my eyes as she starts her poem, something about a tsunami.

"Hey."

Blaire's sand-on-silk voice is right beside me. A second behind it, the warm press of her hands on my shoulders knead them down from my ears. She's only touched me once before, when her hand brushed mine taking the book from me that first day in the library. Just like then, her touch is like a grenade, sending shrapnel ripping through my insides and leaving me gutted and gasping.

"Hey," I answer when I've gained my composure, twisting in my seat to see her.

She's pulled her dark waves up and pinned them into a loose bun on the back of her head. She's changed into a long-sleeved blue top, but I can't tell if she put on a bra for the occasion because she's got a scarf around her neck that hangs over her breasts.

"You're so tight," she says, her fingers massaging deeper.

"This should help with that," the waitress says, back with my drink. She thumps it on the table in front of me and looks at Blaire over my shoulder. "What about you, honey? Something to drink?"

"Just a Diet Coke," she says, releasing me and slipping into the seat on my right. Once the waitress is gone, she pulls her chair closer and leans in. "I'm last tonight. Better for scoring."

"Scoring?"

She gives a loose shrug. "It's pretty random. Every night there are five judges. They score just like in the Olympics, from one to ten based on how much they liked the poem."

"But you said there's no prize money."

Blaire looks at the stage as the first poet finishes and the audience claps. "The bigger slams all offer prizes to attract better known poets, but this is just for the community, so all we're competing for is bragging rights." She smiles up at the waitress as she sets her Coke in front of her, then turns back to me. "And every once in a while, someone gets discovered at one of these things."

A boo goes up from the crowd when the MC starts to read the scores. I turn and see a guy at the bar holding up a 5.5 on his whiteboard. The other scores are in the sevens and eights.

Two more poets perform, and they fare a little better, inching into the nines.

"That's Gloria," Blaire says, pointing at the black woman climbing the stairs to the stage, preparing to perform. "She's really good. She usually wins when she brings something original."

"Doesn't everyone?" I ask, then clarify when she gives me a blank stare. "Isn't every piece performed original poetry?"

She sips her Coke from the straw and nods when she understands what I'm asking. "We all write our own poetry, but most of what you hear is rehashed. Some of them read the same thing over and over for months. That's when the scores really drop, since it's generally the same people here listening each time. If you want to score, you have to bring something fresh, which is why I write something new every month."

"Can't wait to hear it." I can't help but smile at her enthusiasm.

She twirls a tendril of loose hair around her finger and sucks on her straw, her eyes shifting to the woman onstage. My gaze doesn't follow, even though I will it to. I can't take my eyes off the smooth line of her jaw and the curve of her mouth, the nose that turns up slightly at the end. Her whiskey eyes are large and wide-set under arching black brows that flatten at the outer ends. She's exquisite.

Fucking flawless.

"She's done that one before," she says with a scrunch of her nose, turning back to me, and I realize I didn't hear a word the woman onstage uttered.

I reach for my scotch and knock half of it back in one swallow.

Blaire leans her shoulder into mine when I set my glass down and juts her chin at the mousy pubescent boy on the stage, reciting about coming out to his parents. "I'm next. Wish me luck."

"Does break a leg apply in these situations, or is that just cliché?" I ask with a smile.

She smiles back and pushes up from her seat as the boy finishes and the scores go up. "I'll take it."

The MC reads off the scores, all in the mid to high nines, as Blaire waits at the bottom of the stairs. "And last, but certainly not least, we have a crowd favorite," the MC says as Blaire starts up the stairs. "Our very own, Blaire Leon!"

Something inside me prickles when he catches Blaire by the waist on her way by and whispers something in her ear. She smiles and takes her place under the spotlight behind the mic. She takes a deep breath, then steps closer, lifting her head to the audience. Before she's even said a word, there's a whoop from the back of the room, followed by a "You go, girl!" from the poet, Gloria, who's sitting at a front table with a group of others who have already read.

"They tell you when you're a baby not to touch yourself," Blaire starts with consternation on her face and the waggle of a finger. "When you're a teen, they say: Don't look. It's dirty. That website is nasty. And besides, it's not *really* like that. No one actually does that. No one *sounds* like that. It doesn't *feel* like they make it look like it feels."

She lowers her hand and her face softens. "Wait, they say, until you're older. Wait, they say, until you're in love."

Her expression grows into a combination of wary and confused as she lifts a questioning hand, palm up to the audience. "But if sex is dirty, why would I do it with someone I love? If sex is dirty, then didn't we all come from the dirt? What if I like the dirt?"

She pauses, rolls her head to the side and closes her eyes. Her hands smooth down her sides and splay on her thighs. "What if I want to get dirty?"

Her eyes open and search like a beacon through the dark room, locking on mine. She hooks her fingertips under the hem of her short skirt and I feel my cock respond, swelling at the thought of where she's going— and where I'm fucking dying to take her.

"What if I want to roll in the mud until I'm so fucking filthy that I'll never be clean again? Does that make me bad? Nasty? A whore? Does it mean I'll never find love? A life? A man who respects me?"

She lets go of her skirt and her expression hardens. "And what about that man? How dirty is *he*? Does anyone even care if he's caked with mud? Does anyone even notice?"

A strand of long, dark hair springs free when she gives her head an angry shake and cascades down the side of her face, partially covering one eye. "The answer, my friends, is no. He can be filthy and somehow that makes him hotter. It makes all us dirty girls want to get even dirtier with him."

She's heaves a few deep breaths, as if calming herself from the rant she was working herself into. When she continues, there's a rasp of despair in her voice.

"If I like to fuck, and he likes to fuck, how does that make us different? Why do his friends talk about me like a piece of meat when mine talk about him as if he hung the moon? Why do my guys never call again, but his women sext him the second they leave his bed?"

One more deep breath. "When they say it's a man's world, they must be talking about the bedroom. Glass ceilings are shattering. We'll have a female president someday. But only if she's never slept around. Because a male president can get head in the Oval Office, but no goddamn dirty whore is ever going to be good enough to run our country."

She drops her head and steps back from the mic.

There's a second of stunned silence, but a woot from the audience breaks it just before the entire place breaks into thundering applause. Blaire bows with a flourish, then skips off the stage with a smile and wave.

I'm still reeling as I turn to the room and watch the first score go up—the guy in the back who's been tough on everyone tonight. A ten. One 9.9 pops up before two more tens and a 9.6.

I watch her wend her way back to me and my gut reaction is to bolt as the fight or flight reflex takes control. If I understood what she just said, she's down with getting dirty. Filthy. And I want to fucking roll her in the mud so hard I can taste it. But I can't.

Not yet.

She slips back into the seat next to me and pulls off her scarf, hooking an elbow behind the backrest.

And, Christ, this girl is going to be the fucking death of me.

Her shirt is damp with stage sweat and there is definitely no bra. The thin cotton fabric hugs tight nipples at the tips of breasts that aren't big enough to be fake, but are firm and round and a perfect handful.

"What did you think?" she asks a little breathily.

"It was…" I swallow. "Just fucking…wow."

"Not exactly Blake or Byron," she says, trying and failing to hide a cocky smirk. "I don't think Professor Duncan really understood what I was talking about when I said I write poetry."

A smile blooms over my face with the image of Blaire reciting that poem in Dr. Duncan's class. "Poetry's not really about iambic pentameter and rhyming anymore, is it?"

"It is and it isn't." She slips my scotch glass from my fingers and takes a slow sip. I memorize the curve of her neck and the way her throat moves as she swallows. She lowers the glass to the table and watches her index finger trace the rim. I memorize the shape of her hands and her slender fingers tipped in midnight blue polish. "I think that's how we all started and I still enjoy writing that kind of poetry. Traditional poetry is important for teaching us how to craft language. But slam poetry is more about rhythm and execution than actual rhyming and structure." She brushes the errant strand of hair behind her ear. As she lifts her eyes to mine, they sink three layers deeper into me than anyone else's ever have and moor themselves to my soul. "Nothing about slam poetry is timid or restrained. It doesn't speak; it screams."

I close my hand over hers on my glass. "It was incredible. *You* were incredible."

I'm losing myself in her eyes. She's got the power to do that to me—make everything else just fade out until the only thing in my world is her.

"Hey, Blaire!"

The voice rips me out of Blaire and I look up at the MC, standing on her other side.

"You were seriously killing it up here tonight!" he says with a grin. But I don't miss how his eyes slip to me and narrow slightly.

"Thanks," she says.

His eyes move between us. "This your uncle or something?"

My throat constricts.

"Caiden, this is Craig," she says, flipping a hand at him, "the owner's son. Craig, this is my friend, Caiden."

He holds out his hand. I take it and he squeezes more than shakes. "Blaire is something, huh? Had you heard her read before?"

"No, I hadn't, and yes, she is."

Blaire stands. "We've got to go," she says, grabbing her bag from under the table. She starts toward the door and flips a wave behind her. "See you next month, Craig."

I follow but her progress is slow. Everyone wants a piece of her. They've all got a hug or a pat on the back for her, and she seems to know them all by name. I stand to the side, preferring that she doesn't try to introduce me to any more of them and, finally, we make our escape.

Compared to the steamy bar, it's cold when we step outside onto the walk.

"It's freezing out here," she says, wrapping her scarf around her neck, then hugging herself. "You want to get some coffee or something?"

Every fiber in my body wants to wrap itself around her and warm her from the inside out. "Coffee sounds great."

"The Bean is just up the street. If they're still open…"

I take her elbow and we walk in the direction she indicated. "How long have you been performing your poetry?"

"About two years."

"You were really…incredible." I keep struggling for a word that truly captures what I'm trying to say and falling miserably short. "I'd love to hear more of your work."

She wraps her fingers around mine, where they rest lightly on her arm, and smiles. "I'm here every fourth Friday of the month." She presses closer. "Or I could give you a private reading anytime you want."

Her breast is against my arm, doing things to totally unrelated parts of my body. "That would be…" I look at her and her eyes flash a message into mine. My groin hears it, loud and clear.

She turns toward the storefront we're passing. "Damn."

I glance past her and see we're at The Bean. It's dark inside. "No big thing." I look back toward Tino's and see we're near my car, just on the other side of the street. "Where are you parked?"

"About a block past Tino's and around the corner to the left, on Fifth."

"It's cold. My car's right there," I say, pointing at my black Charger. "Let me give you a lift back."

"Okay," she says, stepping into the deserted street.

I click the doors as we cross and she slides into my passenger seat without any hesitation. I might not be an ax murderer, but I'm no less dangerous.

I crank the engine and my latest obsession song pours from the speakers.

"Arctic Monkeys," she says, nodding along to the heavy percussion. "Nice."

I turn down the volume. "Sorry."

She tosses me a wicked smile and cranks the stereo back up.

I adjust the heat and swallow when the song betrays me by telling her I've dreamt about her nearly every night this week, and asks how many secrets she can keep. I pull onto the road and head back toward the bar. "Just tell me when."

She points out the windshield. "At that stop sign, take a left. I'm just a few cars up." I do as I'm told and she points to a silver Mini. "That's me."

"Sweet ride," I say with a nod.

"My dad bought it but he didn't like it, so he gave it to me so he wouldn't have to drive me back and forth to school. Saves him having to pretend we know each other."

I pull into a spot across the street from her car and cut the engine. "You're not close?" I ask, turning in my seat to face her.

She shrugs. "I've never really met him, even though we've lived in the same house all my life."

I try to read her expression, but all I'm finding there is indifference. Either she's great at stuffing down her emotions or she truly doesn't care. Either way, she's better at dealing with family shit than I am. "That's tough."

"Not really. Growing up is a hell of a lot easier when you've got parents that are just phoning it in. I never had to deal with any of the shit my friends did. No groundings. No curfew. I can order a pizza and eat in my room because no one's at the dinner table anyway. I can fuck in my own bed without anyone caring. I do what I want, when I want."

My heart's suddenly pounding in my chest with the image of her fucking. But she must have her head on pretty straight to have made it twenty years in the world on her own compass without landing in jail. "So, I take it you still live at home?"

She nods.

It's not unusual. Sierra State, like most of the California State schools, is predominantly a commuter campus.

"Where is that?"

"Up in the foothills. On county land near Ashby."

"How long does it take you to get home from here?" I ask, suddenly concerned she's driving on her own, even though she didn't drink much.

"It's only a half hour, as long as there's no fog."

"Coffee might have helped," I say with a flick of my wrist in the general direction of The Bean. "Sorry that didn't work out."

"Next time," she says with a smile.

Without realizing I'm doing it, I find I'm leaning toward her. I catch myself and stop. But before I can pull back, she closes the rest of the distance and presses her lips hard against mine.

Any thought that I shouldn't be doing this evaporates like fog in a stiff breeze at the taste of her mouth, moving hungrily on mine. She's scotch and fire on my tongue as she devours me. Right or wrong, I'm powerless to stop her.

Her fingers run down my face to my chest as she opens her mouth wider, inviting me deeper inside. I take the invitation, tasting as much of her as she'll give me. Her hands tug at the hem of my shirt and my breath catches when cold fingers meet my warm abs.

I press harder against her, drawing her closer, and fire rips through my veins as our tongues and hands explore the new landscapes of each other's mouths and bodies.

But a shard of coherent thought finally manages to pierce the bubble I've constructed to justify what I'm doing. "You're a student," I say against her mouth.

Her lips skim to my ear. "I like you, Caiden," she whispers, and her saying my name with that hot breath, that wet mouth, is nearly enough to break my resolve. "I like you a lot."

I take her by the shoulders and gently peel her away, my heart hammering out African drumbeats against my ribcage. "You're so damn incredible, but I can't do this. It's totally against university rules. I'm sorry."

"You're not *my* professor," she says, her expression wounded. "If we like each other, I don't see why it should matter."

"I'm Dr. Duncan's graduate assistant. My boss *is* your professor. It's a conflict of interest, since I do most of his grading."

"So you *are* conflicted." It's clear from the predatory shift her expression takes that she hears that I'm trying to convince myself as much as her.

I drop my head against the headrest. "I am."

She leans closer again, her breast pressing against my arm through the thin cotton of her top. "I'll never say anything. No one needs to know," she whispers, her breath feathering over my neck and stiffening my cock.

My breaths are shallow pants, and I force my lungs to expand with my next inhalation. If I stay in this car with her, so close, I'm going to give in.

"Tonight was really amazing, but I need to get home," I say, cranking the ignition and gluing my palm to the stick shift.

There's a long minute that she doesn't move. Finally, she leans in and presses a kiss to my cheek, then opens her door.

I watch her cross to her car, and when she pulls out, I crank a U-turn and head home. Where I jerk off to Arctic Monkeys with the vivid image of getting dirty with Blaire playing on a loop behind my eyelids.

CHAPTER 3

Blaire

"We finally did it yesterday," my best friend Zoey tells me when she slips into the passenger seat of the Mini.

Her mom waves from the front door as we pull away from the curb.

"Who did what?" I ask and really try to pay attention to the answer.

I was off in space all weekend, putting the milk in the cupboard and the cereal in the fridge. My mind won't turn off, reliving kissing Caiden, planning all the other things I want to do to him.

Once I realized he's as nervous about me as I am about him, the nerves melted away and things somehow became easy between us. We've got so much in common, from our love of literature, to our taste in music, to how he gets my poetry, to things I can't even put my finger on, but feel enormous. Things having to do with how his touch makes my very DNA hum, and the way his glance causes poetry to leak from my soul.

But he's got rules.

Zoey's gaze blazes exasperation into mine as I turn the corner at the end of her block. I feel it like a deathbeam, breaking through my deflector shields. "We had *sex*, Blaire! I finally let Kevin fuck me."

"About damn time. That boy's had blue balls for months."

She shoves my shoulder hard, causing me to jerk the steering wheel and veer us across the oncoming lane, which is thankfully empty, sideswiping the trashcans on the opposite curb. "You are such a bitch!"

"You say that like it's a bad thing," I say, righting the ship.

She shoves her short yellow bob behind her ear and glares out the windshield. "You're supposed to be all, like, 'Oh my God, Zoey! Give me all the deets!'"

"Oh my God, Zoey! Give me all the deets!" I cut her a glare as I take the right out to the main road. "You spend way the hell too much time on social media. You know I'd never actually say 'deets,' right? That's not even a word."

"You should at least have a Snapchat," she grumbles.

"Why? So I can be brainwashed along with the rest of you?"

I boycotted social media in junior high when I discovered it was just hive mentality—a crash course in unoriginal thinking.

She rolls her eyes and drops back into her seat. "Whatever. Just forget it. I'll tell Jessica when we get to school."

"It's not like you cashed in your V-card or anything, Zoe," I say, starting to feel a little guilty. This is what friends are supposed to do, right? Tell each other this shit? "Sorry. I just don't get what the big deal is."

She throws a hand at me. "Your mystery boy must have fucked you wrong, because otherwise you'd *know* what the big deal is."

And...there goes any guilt I might have been feeling. "Bitch."

Zoey's pretty much the only friend I have outside Marcus and Nate, though she's cultivated a wider circle than me. I honestly have never related well to people my age. I can't do the standard fashion critiquing and boy watching that goes on in lunch circles and end up drifting into my own mind, so the rest of Zoey's friends think I'm socially stunted.

Maybe I am. Maybe it's in my genes to not be quite right socially. Or maybe it's what Mrs. Erikson said. Whenever she read anything I wrote last year in English she would say I have an old soul. But Zoey tolerates my social ineptitude. Usually.

I'd been at Marie's since I was a few weeks old, but Zoey started there for preschool and she sort of latched onto me. She cried the second day of public kindergarten when they advanced me to first grade and told her she couldn't come with me. I tell her more than I tell anyone else, but there are some things—okay, a lot of things—that I keep to myself. She knows I lost my virginity last summer. She just doesn't know to who. I told her it was a guy from our rival high school and made up some random name.

I wouldn't have told her anything, except she's been on my case to "just do it" since she fucked Jon Fitzmeyer last spring after prom. I think she just wanted someone who'd been through it to share the gory details with, because after I told her, I heard every detail about Jon. Such as, his penis curves out when he's hard, he doesn't kiss while he's fucking, and he looks like he's having a seizure when he comes. She thinks it's because he's concentrating so hard.

She's been dating Kevin since the beginning of the school year. They've traded oral, but that's it.

"He's bigger than Jon, in case you care," she says huffily, her arms crossed over her chest. "Not longer, but thicker. I felt it stretch more."

"I'll remember that for when I'm fucking him," I say, turning up the radio. It's Caiden's Arctic Monkey's song from last night. Zoey pissed me off when she said Nate fucked me wrong, so she doesn't get to dump all her shit on me now.

She glares at me. "I just thought you might find it interesting. You never really know what a guy is packing."

I turn onto the street that leads up the hill to school. "You've sucked Kevin's dick, and you're just now discovering it's different than Jon's?"

"Jesus, B! What the fuck is with you today?"

Fucking Caiden, that's what. He's got me so hot and bothered that I can't think straight. And talking to Zoey about having sex isn't helping. I appreciate what Nate and I have even more now, because he's never left me feeling this sexually frustrated.

"Sorry. I'm just in a shitty mood," I admit, hoping she won't ask why.

"Well, you don't need to bring me down with you." There's my Zoey. Always the narcissist.

"Sorry," I say again. "So, tell me everything."

She does, and by the time we climb out of my car in the school lot, I know more about Kevin's junk than I ever wanted to. But as I walk to first period calculus, I can't help wondering what Caiden might be packing.

I'm particularly vicious in water polo practice this afternoon. Near the end, I take a shot that leaves our goalie with a bloody nose.

Coach Jackson gives me a pat on the back on the way to the locker room. "Great work out there, Leon." He likes a little blood in the water, so his comment doesn't surprise me. "You sure you don't want me reaching out to college coaches? It's late for Division One schools, but there are some great D2's that would piss themselves to sign you."

"Thanks coach, but my plans are Stanford or Berkeley."

"Hell," he says, rubbing his bald head. "They'd take you walk-on, sure as shit. Let me see what I can do."

"I really want to focus on academics," I say, toweling off my hair. "But thanks."

I slip through the locker room door before he can press his argument and head for the shower to get ready for my night class.

And Caiden.

On my way to Sierra State, I pull into the McDonald's next to campus and take in my duffel. I order a Coke and a chicken caesar salad, and when I'm done eating, I take my duffel to the bathroom. I tug off my jeans and sweater and slip on a short black cotton skirt and snug white long-sleeved top. I'd never wear this at school—mostly because I'm invisible there and like it that way—but Caiden kissed me. We were so close to doing more. I pull my sweater on over my shirt, reapply my mascara, brush my teeth, then head to the car.

I tough it out for as long as I can, but knowing Caiden is just two buildings over, in the library, is enough to drive me to distraction. Professor Duncan's an okay guy, so I feel guilty about cutting out of his class early, but as I stare at my blank notebook, I know there's no point being here anyway. Before I reach the doors of the library, I unhook my bra and pull it out through my sleeve, then tug off my sweater and shove them both in my messenger bag. I take a deep breath for nerves, then climb the stairs to the fifth floor resource center.

Caiden is at the desk, and a blond girl is leaning on the counter, pushing her cleavage all up in his face. When I see him smile at her, flirting back, jealousy chokes up my throat. I swallow it along with the acid rising and berate myself. Jealousy is not my thing. And besides, he's not mine.

Yet.

I watch from the corner of my eye as he notices me and watches as I cross to the back of the reference section. I drop my bag on the table and pull out *Don Juan*, then sit and cross my legs slowly.

With all my swimming, I've got great legs. They'd always been my best asset, until the rest of my body finally caught up this summer. I run a hand over my thigh, lifting the hem of my skirt just a little higher, as I open my book.

"Hey," Caiden's smooth timbre comes from just behind me.

I look up and catch his eyes on my legs before they lift to my face. The blonde at the desk is gone. "Hey."

He gives a quick glance around the library, then slides into the seat next to me. "I wanted to apologize for what happened on Friday." His eyes drop to the tabletop, where his finger is tracing nervous circles. "It won't happen again, but if you feel the need to report me to Dr. Duncan or the university, I'd totally understand."

A laugh escapes on a breath before I can contain it. "For what? *I* kissed *you*."

He tips his head and his eyes pour heat into mine. "I was a *very* willing participant, Blaire," he says, low. Secret.

His tone and the hungry look in his eyes cause my insides to ache.

There's a long minute that we just sit here staring at each other, the charge in the air between us building to critical mass and prickling goose bumps all over my body. The storm in his eyes intensifies, darkening the steely blue to nearly black and tightening my groin. He watches as I stand and move toward the stacks behind our table. I turn the corner and lean against the shelves in the first row, out of his line of sight—and anyone else's for that matter. I wait for a century, it feels like, breathing my erratic heartbeat back into rhythm. When he doesn't follow, disappointment pools inside me. I was sure I saw something in his gaze.

I'm just deciding my seduction tactic failed when he turns the corner of the shelves and stares at me from the end. "What are we playing here, Blaire? Hide and seek?"

I spin and pretend to be looking over the books on the shelf in front of me, suddenly feeling like a stupid little girl. "I'm using the reference section of the library. Not sure what *you're* doing."

I don't look as he moves behind me, but I feel him there in the crackle of the air and the way it makes all the hairs on my arms stand on end.

"Hmm..." He stands close and looks over my shoulder. "What other classes are you taking this semester?" he asks, running a finger along the spines. "Because I've seen Dr. Duncan's syllabus and I know for certain he didn't assign anything on Aristotle or Socrates."

I shift a little and my backside brushes against the front of his pants. "Maybe I'm reading on my own— expanding my horizons and trying someone new."

A rush shudders through me when he doesn't pull away. I press my ass tighter against him and feel a bulge behind his zipper.

Knowing that he wants me as much as I want him is exhilarating. It makes me bolder. He stands rock steady, coiled tight and not even breathing, as I start to move my ass against him. After a minute, he lays his hands on my hips and presses his whole front against my whole back.

"This is so wrong," he whispers into my hair.

I lay my hands over his so he won't take them off me as I turn slowly in his arms. "Why?"

He tips his head back and stares at the ceiling for several beats of my racing heart. I take the opportunity to study the V of his collarbones and the curve of his Adam's apple as he swallows. Finally, he lowers his gaze to mine. "I'm not even going to tell you all the ass I've had to kiss and the mountain of debt I've buried myself under to get this far, but I've been at this university for seven years." His fingers dig into my hips. "If we do this..." He trails off and bites his lips into a line with a sharp shake of his head, then blows out a shaky breath and lets me go. "There's a reason for University policies," he says, backing away a step. "I can't take the risk. I'm sorry, Blaire." He backs away another step and the storm in his eyes ravages me as hurricane Caiden sweeps over my body. "You have no idea how sorry."

He spins and the next second, he's gone.

I lean against the shelves and tip my head back, catching the breath that he just stole from me. The empty ache in my chest rivals the hot aching need low in my belly. My mind is spinning, grasping desperately for anything that might change his mind. I could drop poetry class...add a literature class that Professor Duncan doesn't teach.

But I don't think that would be enough. And if he finds out I'm still in high school...

I've been at this university for seven years.

He's not twenty-two. If my math is right, which I can't guarantee based on my current state of mind, he's at least twenty-four.

Guilt cramps my insides and I breathe into my toes to flush it out. I should just walk away. That's clearly what he wants me to do.

I take another deep breath, then collect myself and turn the corner into the open area between the shelves and the resource desk. My heart skips when I see Caiden behind the counter. Across from him with his back to me is my tweed clad professor. Caiden's eyes lock on mine over Professor Duncan's shoulder. In them, I see everything I'm feeling: desire, despair. But where I'm feeling doubt, what I see in his gaze is determination. His mind is made up.

Whatever we were starting is over.

His gaze turns back to Professor Duncan and I go to the table and gather my things. I cross the room and shuffle down the stairs without looking back.

CHAPTER 4

Caiden

My hand hesitates with the envelope perched at the lip of the mailbox. I pull it back and stare at the address, wondering for the thousandth time why I do this.

Especially this month.

It's Mom's mortgage or my rent. I don't have enough student loan money to cover both. Hopefully my landlord's on another binge. That might give me until my next work-study check comes on the tenth before he realizes I'm late.

My loving mother kicked me out of the house for good five years ago, on Christmas day, in the middle of my sophomore year at Sierra. Said she couldn't stand the sight of me anymore. Maybe it was because I'm Dad's spitting image. More likely, she blamed me for the train wreck her life had become. I guess, in a backdoor sort of way, what happened *was* my fault.

When my younger brother, Chris, stood up for me, she threw him out too. There were a few crazy weeks where my thirteen-year-old brother and I lived in my car. I tried to get ahold of Dad for help, but by that time he was months behind on Chris's child support and no one knew where his mid-life crisis had carried him. Once school started again in January, I'd drop Chris off at the junior high early and he'd shower and eat breakfast there before class. I withdrew from classes, moved out of the dorms, and used my student loan to get us a cheap hotel room and keep us fed.

But I knew the money was going to run out. And living in limbo wasn't helping either of us.

So I went home when Chris was at school one day and had it out with Mom. I told her she needed to pull her shit together because Chris still needed somewhere to live. She told me I was a useless piece of shit. I told her Chris wasn't. She finally agreed and I dropped him back at home that night.

He thought I chose school over him. Hated me for a long time for that.

I found my fleabag apartment that summer and started funneling what I was saving on the dorms to him so he'd have decent clothes and whatever. He still crashed at my place all through high school when things got bad at home. He just graduated in May and officially moved in here when he started JC in the fall.

Which means I don't need to pay Mom's mortgage anymore. Chris doesn't need her. I should give that money to him so he doesn't have to accept so many student loans.

I hate the thought of him getting buried under them the way I have.

I run my fingers over the envelope. Even if Mom knew I've been covering the mortgage since the foreclosure notice came four years ago, she wouldn't appreciate it. She'd probably say I was doing it out of guilt.

Who knows? Maybe I am. Whatever the reason, the thought of her losing the home I grew up in sits worse with me than finding a way to keep her there.

The car behind me honks. I lift my eyes to the rearview and honk back, then shove the envelope in the slot and peal away from the curb.

When I reach campus, I go straight to the Student Wellness building and change in the locker room. Jones is stretching against the wall when I get to the kickboxing mats.

"You're late."

I shrug as I pull on my gloves. "It happens."

"Watched *Fight Night* this weekend," he says with a grin as he tugs on a glove and ties it. "Learned some new moves. Prepare to be dazzled."

"Should have brought my sunglasses."

I finish tying my gloves and press in my mouth guard as I take my spot on the mat. When Jones is done fussing with his gear, he joins me.

I strike out with a right hook followed by a knee to the hip and take him to the mat.

"Holy hell, Brenner," he grumbles through his mouth guard. "I thought we were warming up. What the fuck crawled up your ass?"

"You name it," I say, hooking an elbow into his and hauling him up.

"Duncan?"

"Among other things." Like a tight little undergrad who's still featured in my dreams every night.

He comes at me with an uppercut that I deflect before landing one of my own. I jam my knee into his ribs and follow it with a jab to the gut.

He doubles over and backs away, spitting out his mouth guard and glaring up at me. "It's that tight piece of ass from the library, isn't it?"

"What the hell are you talking about?"

"You know exactly what *who* I'm talking about," he says, popping in the guard. He brings a knee up, connecting with my ribs. "You ran me off for a reason."

I dodge to the left as his fist comes at my face. "You know I can't go there."

"Which explains all this pent up, high-velocity angst."

I pummel him with another barrage of uppercuts and send him to the floor with a kick to his side. Because the prick is right. I'm frustration personified, blindly annihilating anything in my path. Unfortunately for him, he's in my path at the moment. So I picture his face when he was getting ready to make his move on Blaire, then duck and punch, sidestep and kick.

Because one second I've got myself convinced that I can follow through—that we only have to keep it hidden for four months. And the second after that I'm asking myself: What the fuck am I doing?

So far the only answer I've come up with is "fucking my future straight to hell."

But, Christ. This girl stood on stage a week ago and blew my mind. I can't stop thinking about the power of her poem. She owned it—her love of sex and her hate of the double standard. She put it all right out there without reservation.

She's got to be the bravest fucking woman I've ever met.

And she wants to get dirty.

I shake the thought out of my head as Jones comes at me with a right hook. She's going to have to get dirty with someone other than me, because we can't happen.

Part of me was satisfied that she'd gotten my message when she didn't come to the library after class on Wednesday. A bigger part of me was in agony, wanting to run to the lit building to catch at least a glimpse of her walking to her car. But that part can't have what it wants. Too much is at risk.

When Jones lifts his hands an hour later and breathes, "No más," I shower and head over to the lit building. The elevator takes a day to come after I punch the button, so I finally give up and climb the stairs to the third floor two at a time. I try Dr. Duncan's office, but it's locked. Probably at lunch. I turn up the hall toward the bank of faculty mailboxes to check if he left anything in my box that needs handling. There's nothing but a note from him reminding me the next chapter of my dissertation is due a week from today.

Fuck. I haven't even started pulling my thoughts together yet.

Usually after a workout I feel more focused, but right now, everything inside me is a mass of chaos—a thousand pin balls ricocheting off every surface. Instead of dissipating, all that kinetic energy is escalating to critical mass.

I'm going to fucking blow apart at the seams.

"You look more wound up than I am. And that's saying something."

I turn at the familiar voice and find Hannah standing behind me. Her long blond hair is up in a high ponytail and she's dressed professionally, in a teal silk blouse and a black pencil skirt. Her heels bring her to my six foot one. "You look good. Presentation this morning?"

She nods and lifts a hand to rub her shoulder under the strap of her bag. "Just finished my proposal meeting with the dissertation board."

"Great. How'd it go?"

"They signed off on it this time, so thank fucking God."

I shove Dr. Duncan's note in my pocket and hike my messenger bag higher on my shoulder. "I was heading over to the library for my shift, but I've got a few minutes if you want to get some lunch or whatever."

A smile tugs at her mouth and one blond eyebrow arches. "I'm too jacked up to eat right now, but I'd be definitely be up for 'whatever.'"

My eyes take a long drink of her body. This might be exactly what I need. "Yeah. I could do that."

She turns up the hall and I follow her to her faculty advisor's office. She slips the key in the lock and opens the door. "Dr. Garret's in class until two."

She leaves the light off as I step in behind her and she locks the door. She unbuttons her blouse. It falls to the floor in a teal puddle at her feet as she reaches behind her for the clasp of her bra.

It takes me a minute to catch up. I tug off my shirt and toss it on the arm of the wingchair next to Dr. Garret's desk. I toe off my Vans and socks, and by the time I'm shucking my jeans down my legs, she's already down to a nude lace thong and her heels. She reaches into her bag for a condom, then takes my hand and tows me to Dr. Garret's side of the desk. She slips her panties down her legs and slides her ass onto the desk, then pulls me between her knees and tugs my boxer briefs over my erection. I watch as she sheathes my cock in latex.

Then I ram it into her.

She leans back onto her hands and rolls her neck in a circle, unwinding some of the tension there. "I needed this so bad."

Me too. I need a distraction from the incredibly fuckable but very off-limits undergrad giving me the worst case of blue balls I've ever had.

I grasp Hannah's hips and pull her right to the edge of the desk, then drive into her over and over. My thumb searches out her clit and I work it with our rhythm.

"Fuck, yes," she groans, closing her eyes.

For the next several minutes, there's grunting and gasping and the slapping of skin. When she arches up and opens her mouth in a silent prayer, I let myself go, knowing she's got what she needed.

"You know, most men aren't as attentive as you to a woman's needs," she says as I'm tugging off the condom. "You're the only guy I've ever been with who waits to be sure I have mine first."

"It's only fair," I say, wrapping it in tissue and burying it under papers in Dr. Garret's trash.

She blows out a derisive laugh. "I wish they all saw it that way."

I tug up my boxers. "I've never seen it any other way."

I was a late bloomer, I suppose. I lost my virginity first semester of my freshman year in college. Veronica was a twenty-one-year-old senior sociology major. And she was a nymphomaniac.

We met on the track at the student fitness center on a Tuesday afternoon. By Tuesday night, I was in her bed and never got out until the following Monday morning. Unbeknownst to my parents, I moved into her apartment the following week and my dorm roommate never saw me again until the day I came to collect the rest of my crap at the end of the school year.

I'm convinced I had more sex that year than most guys do in a lifetime. We fucked like rabbits—five or six times a day. Every day. But Veronica had one rule—sex etiquette, she called it: *The guy isn't done until the girl comes.* She taught me more about female anatomy than I ever learned in human sexuality freshman year. She taught me exactly what to do with my tongue and my fingers and my cock to make it good for the girl.

I think I might have fallen a little in love with Veronica that year. I was certainly infatuated with her. We kept in touch for a few months after she graduated, but she moved to Manhattan for bigger and better things and that was that.

I've had enough opportunity since Veronica to keep my skills sharp, but I've never had a serious relationship since. Not that I'm not looking for The One. I think deep down, everyone is. But so far, no one's hit the mark. I think it's just one of those things. I'll know her when I see her. Not like love at first sight. I don't really believe in that. But I keep telling myself that when I find her, there'll be something about her that's different. Something that I can't get anywhere else. Something about her will speak to me in a way no one else ever has.

Hannah and I finish dressing and slip out of Dr. Garret's office. I watch her walk away with her heels dangling from her fingers, nearly six feet of instant relief.

We don't do this very often—only four or five times in the two years we've been in the program together—but there are times a guy just needs a fuckbuddy.

❖

It's been two weeks since I've seen Blaire and I finally feel in control for the first time since she crashed into my life like a speeding comet. I just needed to work off some of the tension. I'm thinking with the right head now. I can maintain appropriate boundaries.

This is where my head is until Blaire appears at the top of the stairs. And that's the instant I know I was dead wrong.

She's in black leggings and a snug white long-sleeved top with a deep V neckline.

And no fucking bra. Christ, don't they sell underwear in her town?

I'm momentarily breathless, and totally helpless to take my eyes off her.

She watches me watching her as she saunters toward me and leans on the counter. "I was hoping you'd have time to work through some Byron with me."

My brain scrambles, synapses firing at random. "I'm pretty busy," I stammer. "Got another chapter of my dissertation due to Dr. Duncan on Friday, so…"

"What's it on?" she asks, leaning against the counter.

I'm finally able to breathe and I take a second to do that before answering. "It's actually pretty dry. Don't think you'd find it all that interesting."

"Because I'm too stupid to grasp your lofty literary concepts?" she says, a scowl clouding her flawless features.

I lean onto the counter between us and shake my head. "I sincerely doubt there's anything you're too stupid to grasp, Blaire."

"So?" she says with an inquisitive tip of her head. "Lay it on me."

I take a deep breath. "It's not a mistake Dr. Duncan sent you to me when you decided to do your project on Byron's *Don Juan*. My dissertation is a comparative study of several different international translations in the era it was written and the social impact they had in those regions."

"Social impact?" she asks, arching her eyebrows.

"When Byron wrote the first two cantos of *Don Juan*, it was criticized and nearly banned in certain languages for its 'immoral content.' It wasn't until the third canto published that it began to catch on." I lift my eyes to her. "You've read the first two cantos."

She nods. "Donna Julia, who's twenty-three and married, seduces a sixteen-year-old Don Juan."

I pin my eyes to her face, because, if left to their own devices, they'd be devouring her body. Her clothes hug every contour and leave little to the imagination. "That was pretty risky thinking for the early 1800s."

"But not so risky now," she says, leaning closer, her fingertips overlapping mine.

"But still not socially acceptable, either," I counter, stepping back and leaning against the desk behind me in an attempt to create some much needed space between me and my temptation.

"So your dissertation and my project dovetail," she says. "You're studying the social impact of Don Juan's sexual conquests, and I'm studying his conflict because of them. If there was no social stigma to having sex, he'd have nothing to feel conflicted about, so they tie directly together."

I have no answer, because in a lot of ways, she's right.

"If you follow that to its logical conclusion," she continues, "all our sexual hang ups stem from socially dictated morals that may not even apply in any given situation. Sex isn't dirty. It's just that some societies have brainwashed generations to believe that, to keep their second graders from masturbating in class."

A smile tugs at my mouth. "I think your poem spoke very nicely to that," I say, unable to help myself.

She smiles back, and there's something decidedly suggestive in it. "I've got more where that came from, any time you're ready for that private reading."

I hang my head between my shoulders and breathe. Once. Twice. Three times. Finally the buzz in my groin fades. Blaire's mind comes at things from a totally different starting point, and she obviously doesn't pull any punches in her poetry. I have a sudden burning need to hear her poems—to hear that mind at work. To know every intimate detail.

"After the end of the semester," I say without looking up, "I'm all yours."

When I hear Dr. Duncan's signature throat clear, my head snaps up, and he's standing across the counter with a folder in his hands. He looks at me over the top of his wire rim glasses, strands of his gray comb-over falling onto his forehead. I glance past him and find Blaire sliding into a seat at her regular table.

"These are pop essays I had the students write in class tonight," he says, handing the folder to me. "There's no rush grading them, but if you can get them back to me by the end of the week, that would be most appreciated."

I take the folder and try to read his expression. What did he hear? "No problem."

"How's that chapter coming? Any new insights?"

"Yeah. I think I've worked out the inconsistencies I was finding in the French literature. There are a few different translations that are all era appropriate."

He combs a hand through his hair, capturing the stray stands and forcing them into compliance. "You could make the argument that the most widely circulated is the translation of record and use regression to determine how much of the data you've collected can be contributed to the other."

The entire time he's speaking, my eyes are glued to Blaire.

"Yeah, that would be easiest," I answer, only half knowing what I'm agreeing to.

"And probably most accurate."

"I'll get to these this weekend," I say, waving the folder in the air.

He reaches over the counter and claps me on the shoulder. "Rumor has it there might be an adjunct position opening in the Literature Department next year. Since you'll have your terminal degree by summer, I could write you a recommendation, if you'd be interested. It's not a guarantee, but at least you know you'd get the interview."

My attention snaps back to him. "Yes. I'd definitely be interested. Thank you, sir."

I'd pictured myself in the trenches, fighting for guest lecture spots at community colleges. Table scraps. But this…an adjunct position at a state university. I wouldn't have to relocate and I'd have a steady paycheck.

"Righty-oh, then." He turns for the elevators. "I'll look for those essays next week."

Once he's gone, I cross to Blaire. "What did he hear?"

"Nothing. I saw him step off the elevator and I came over here."

I breathe out a relieved sigh. "Listen, Blaire. You know I find you fascinating, but I really can't do what we're doing. We've started something that I can't finish."

I don't drop my gaze as she scrutinizes it, looking for the lie. Instead, I set my resolve and let it shine through my eyes.

After a long moment, she nods. "Okay."

"I'm sorry," I say again. "I wish things were different."

I leave it at that. I'm not going to go all "maybe someday" on her. There's no denying we have an electric attraction, but I know from experience that sort of thing flickers out over time. By the end of the semester in three and a half months, we'll both have moved on. No sense making promises now that neither of us will be interested in keeping when the time comes.

A smile ticks at one corner of her mouth. "Me too."

She gathers her things and I watch after her as she turns and walks toward the stairs. When she disappears at the landing, I breathe a sigh of relief.

Bullet dodged.

CHAPTER 5

Blaire

Nate rolls off me, breathing hard. There's a farting sound as our sweat-slick chests unsuction. It's only the middle of March, so it's still pretty cold out, especially after dark. Nate left the engine running and the heater blowing full blast when we climbed into the backseat of his Jeep. In hindsight, that probably wasn't necessary.

"Did you come, baby girl?" he pants.

"Yeah," I lie.

He settles onto his back and I roll on my side, wedging myself between his bulk and the backrest.

He hooks his arm around my neck and presses his face to the crown of my head. "I couldn't wait to get home to you."

He texted yesterday telling me he was coming home for his Mom's fiftieth birthday party, which is tomorrow, I guess. Said he'd be in town by eight and I should meet him at the high school. It was the first time I'd heard from him since he left my bed two months ago at the end of winter break.

I guess since Marcus isn't home he didn't want to come to my house and fuck me there.

"I fucking missed you," he breathes into my hair.

I look up at him. "Don't you mean you missed fucking me?"

He gives me that full-dimple smile. "All of the above." I settle into his side and his fingers brush over my back. "Marcus said you got into Stanford."

"And Berkeley," I say. "I'm going there."

"Damn, girl." I can tell he's grinning even though I'm not looking at his face. "Maybe some of those brains will rub off on me."

"Probably not," I say.

He chuckles and gropes my ass.

As I lay here, it hits me how achingly empty I feel. This isn't how it was the first two times we had sex. I guess that's because I didn't have any expectations other than being wanted for a few minutes. But now I want Caiden. I want the all-consuming aching need that being near him makes me feel. I want the palpable connection that crackles between us when we're together—how it feels like we're touching sometimes even when we're feet apart.

Or maybe it's passion I want.

All I know is, whatever it is I need now, Nate isn't giving it to me.

Nate's hand combs through my hair and I try to convince myself this is enough. I try to be happy with what I've got. He's still a hundred times better than any of the trolls at school. I close my eyes and sink into his warmth.

But just as I'm starting to get comfortable, he sits up. "I gotta get home. Told Mom I'd be there tonight." He shucks off the condom and drags his jeans over his hips and buttons them, then pulls his phone out of the pocket. "She's been blowing up my phone the whole time we were fucking."

I sit next to him and grab my underwear and leggings off the floorboards. "You should have gone home first."

His smile is cocky when he turns it on me and slips a hand between my legs. "No way you weren't going to be my first stop, baby girl."

We tug our clothes on and I push out the back door as he slips over the back of the driver's seat. We're parked behind the high school, in the faculty lot, which is empty this time of night. I don't bother to ask if I'll see him again before he goes back to school. I don't think I want to. I don't even know why I'm doing this except that I've spent the last five weeks and four days trying to honor Caiden's wishes to stay the hell away from him. I thought seeing Nate might distract me from counting days…hours. I thought it might kill the burning ache in my chest every time I force my feet to carry me to the student parking lot after class instead of the library. I've got to stop wishing for Caiden's hands on me, because he made it pretty clear it's not going to happen again. I guess I hoped someone else's hands on me might quell the need.

Nate's backing out of his spot before I'm even in my car. He honks as he peals out onto the road.

I drop into my seat and head home.

CHAPTER 6

Caiden

Blaire has stopped tormenting me. There were six weeks that I didn't see her at all after our talk at the end of January. About five weeks ago, she started coming into to the library again when she needed me to help interpret something she'd read. We sit and work it out at the resource desk. But she's stopped flinging sexual innuendo at me with every other breath. When she's here, I keep my hands splayed on the counter as to avoid any accidental brushes or any hint of impropriety.

I start the interview process for the adjunct faculty position next week and my moral character cannot be in question. I need to be above reproach.

But in private, all bets are off. I don't even want to know how many hundreds of millions of my potential future children I've washed down the shower drain or scrubbed out of my boxers and sheets.

I'm just bundling them into a pillow case to wash in the dorm laundry for the third time this week when I realize Chris is on the foldout in the family room. Technically he still lives with me, but he has a girlfriend at school he crashes with most nights.

No one drew the shades so the late morning sun is beating in on him. I drop my sheets near the door and go to the kitchen for my morning caffeine.

It's halfway through percolating when Chris's head lifts from under his pillow. "I'm fucking begging you, Bro," he says, his voice coarse with sleep. He holds out his arm. "Hook the IV up and just mainline it."

I pull the carafe and pour two mugs, then bring one over to him. The fact that he looks much more like Mom than I do—dishwater blonde hair and eyes bluer than mine, with her thin face and fair skin—didn't save him. As far as Mom's concerned, he still bears the cross of the dreaded Y chromosome.

"Didn't hear you come in," I say, handing him the mug.

He pulls himself up and leans against the back of the couch before taking it. "It was late. Taryn got a little pissed at me last night."

I rub a hand down my face and look at him. "What happened?"

He downs most of the contents of his mug in two huge swallows, then balances it on the arm of the couch. "That's the thing I don't really get. We were…you know." He gives me a meaningful look. "She started crying in the middle and everything I said just made it worse until she was screaming at me to get out."

I lower myself onto the arm of the couch, wondering why I asked. I'm about the last person who should be giving relationship advice. "Just tell me there's no chance she's pregnant or anything."

He holds up his hands. "No glove no love, man. I'm a firm believer in suiting up."

I know Chris lost his virginity way younger than I did. I had "the talk" with him when he was fourteen. Glad to hear he got my message, which was basically: Be safe. The first time I found a used condom in the trash when I got home from school he was only sixteen.

"Things have been good between you?" I ask after a long swallow. The coffee burns on its way down, just the way I like it.

"Yeah." He looks down at his mug as he swirls the contents. "I really think there's something happening, you know? She's..." He shakes his head. "She's fucking amazing." His face screws into a grimace. "Except when she's screaming at me to get out of her apartment."

"Then maybe that's what you should tell her...the part about her being amazing."

"I did," he says, meeting my gaze. "I told her I loved her."

"Last night?"

He nods.

"For the first time?"

He nods again.

"So, maybe that's the conversation you need to have with her. I don't know what to tell you, but sounds like Taryn does."

"You think I freaked her out?"

"It's possible." I push off the arm of the sofa, downing the last of my coffee. I drop the mug next to the sink. "You don't have class this morning?"

He swings around and sits on the edge of the bed, rubbing a hand over his short hair. "Not until eleven."

"Any laundry you need done?" I ask with a nod at my pile.

He shakes his head. "Taryn took care of me."

I grab my sheets and tug open the door. "Let me know how it goes."

"You'll know it ain't good if I'm back here tonight." He arches his back and rubs the small of it. "Forgot how bad this fold-out blows."

"Later," I say, closing the door behind me.

My little brother's in love. I'm seriously happy for him, but I'm also jealous as hell. If I'm honest with myself, I've known from the minute I met her that it would be easier to fall in love with Blaire than not to.

But falling in love isn't an option.

No one else is in the resource area at eight o'clock on a Friday. I've got my laptop open, pecking out the next chapter of my dissertation on my faulty keyboard when, out of the blue, it feels like a nuclear bomb goes off in my brain. I lose my train of thought mid-sentence, and no matter how many times I read what I started, I can't figure out where I was going with it. I stare at my computer screen, all circuits scrambled, and when I can't even begin to remember what I was trying to say, I swivel my chair toward the room.

And find Blaire on the other side of the counter.

Time freezes and my mangled thoughts focus on one thing. That flawless face. And now I recognize that it was her scent—something warm with the barest hint of sweet, like vanilla—that fried my brain. Spring break was last week and now that we're well into April, the weather is starting to warm. Her long sleeves and leggings are gone, replaced by soft cotton tank tops and tiny skirts.

"Do you have a minute?" she asks, holding up her copy of *Don Juan*.

"Yeah, sure," I say, recovering enough of my composure to speak reasonably coherently. I push up from my chair and move to the counter. "What's up?"

"I'm a little stuck."

"On...?"

She sets the book between us. "In canto five, Don Juan won't sleep with the sultana Gulbeyaz because he's still hung up on Haidee, but in canto nine, he fucks Catherine II. They were both essentially queens and Gulbeyaz was only twenty-six and gorgeous, right? So why the conflict there, and not with the fifty-year-old Catherine?"

"It's your interpretation Dr. Duncan is interested in hearing, not mine, but by the time Juan meets Catherine, you have to remember he's a little older and has been through a war. His perspective on life has changed."

"So, no big deal, screwing an empress," she says with a flip of her hand.

I shrug. "I guess not."

She grabs a handful of hair and tugs in frustration. "It's hard to analyze Don Juan's sexual conflict when it's so damn inconsistent."

I push out of my chair and lean on the counter. "His conflict is going to evolve with time and experience, just like everything else."

She looks at me, all frustration.

"Come here," I say. "There's a really good biography on Byron that might help."

She stands and follows me into the stacks, but we're only a few steps in when she slips in front of me, blocking my path.

"What about *your* sexual conflict, Caiden?" She trails a finger down my bicep. "Any chance that's evolved with time?"

I close my eyes and breathe, but it's no use. Somewhere in the back of my mind, I justify it by telling myself we only have to hide our relationship for a few weeks. After she graduates in a month, there's nothing holding us back.

When she takes my face in both hands and brings it to hers, my last shred of resolve snaps. I yank her to me, one hand on that perfect round ass and the other behind her neck. I destroy her mouth with mine, our teeth grinding and lips tearing. I'm halfway down her throat, trying desperately to claw my way right inside her.

I slide a hand under her top and find the warm mound of her breast. She moans into my mouth when I flick the nipple with my finger before rolling it under the pad of my thumb. Her hands glide over the skin at the waistband of my jeans and I feel my cock lengthen out from underneath it to find her hand. I want to feel those fingers wrapped around me, stroking and pulling.

When she realizes what's happened, that I'm right there trying to force my way under the waistband, she hooks her fingers underneath the layers of my clothing and gives a tug, and I spring out from under my boxer briefs. I groan as she rubs her palm over the exposed inches of my growing cock.

I have to know what she feels like. The impulse is sudden and strong. Base and necessary to my survival, like my need for oxygen. I slip my hand under her skirt, over baby soft skin, and cup her bare ass in my palm.

She grinds herself against me.

I hook my thumb under the cord of the thong between her ass cheeks and glide my hand between her legs from behind. She lifts her leg and rests her foot on the lower shelf of the stacks she's got me pinned against, giving my fingers more room to explore. I push my hand deeper between her legs and find all the wet heat there. I drive my fingers into her core and she drops her head back and moans.

I capture her mouth with mine to swallow the sound. She rocks her hips as I finger her, never letting up on my cock. I draw out and press her away just enough to get my hand between us. I find her clit and stroke it with slick fingers. She shudders hard in my arms, so I stroke again, then press in a circle.

Despite the arousal I see taking over her expression, her gasps and moans, she doesn't forget about me. Her fingers flick open the button of my jeans and our mouths grind as her hand slips down the front of my pants, wriggling under the waistband of my boxer briefs.

And then she has all of me. As her fingers curl around me and she strokes my length, it's like an out-of-body experience. I feel her so intensely that the enormity of the sensation fills the room.

Our tongues continue to do battle and a line of spittle trickles from our chins down my neck. I suck her tongue deep when she strokes me, tip to root, then back.

She rolls her palm over the tip of my cock, catching the pre-cum there, and goes back to work, stroking me right to the edge. When her hand glides lower and cups my balls, they pull tight. I roll her clit harder under my fingers as she drives me over the edge. With one last stroke, she has me coming in my pants like some pubescent boy.

She cries out with her climax and I smother the sound with a slow, deep kiss.

I was a fucking fool to think I could stop this. She's crack and I'm totally addicted.

I pull my hand out and press my forehead to hers. "Well, that was interesting."

"You feeling less sexually conflicted?" she breathes.

I can't stop the smile. "Actually, no. But definitely much less sexually *frustrated*."

She smiles back, letting go of my cock, and bringing her hand to her mouth. She licks the smear of cum off her palm. "You taste good."

And *fuck me*, I'm swelling for her again. I lift my hand to my mouth and suck her juices off my fingers. "You taste better."

She kisses me, and I taste the heady mix of our arousal on each other's tongues. I want so much more from this woman than stolen moments in the library.

But I've already stolen too many tonight. I look down at myself and zip and button my jeans. "You have to stop doing this to me while I'm working. Cum stains aren't easy to hide."

"So, let me see you when you're not working."

I kiss her. "That's probably a very bad idea."

She gives me a devious smile and arches a perfect black eyebrow. "I'm a very bad girl."

Sparklers ignite under my skin and it's everything I can do to force myself to back away. If I wasn't sure before, there's no doubt now. I was never in control. It was always her.

CHAPTER 7

Blaire

Zoey was right. About everything.

I laid in bed last night reliving every moment of what happened in the library with Caiden. Nate was definitely fucking me wrong, because I didn't feel anything close to what Caiden made me feel. And Caiden and I didn't even have actual sex.

She was also on target about guys' packages coming in all shapes and sizes. I'm not stupid. I knew they weren't all the same. What I didn't know is they could be so *big*.

Caiden's hard-on came right out the top of his pants. By inches. He's long and thick. As in, I don't know if he's going to fit long and thick. But he's also perfect— straight, smooth, and circumcised. He felt so hot and hard in my hand, like steel under silk.

I'd never tasted cum before, but I had to taste his.

School almost killed me today. I couldn't concentrate so I don't even want to see my calculus test score. And it's Thursday, so I won't see Caiden tonight.

But tomorrow is the fourth Friday in April, so I'm going to invite him to the poetry slam again.

When I finish my homework, I pull open my laptop and open YouTube. I've never given head before. I've never wanted to. But Caiden makes me want to do *everything*. I type in "blow job," and watch clips of girls with dildos giving instructions.

I want to make Caiden feel good. I want to drive him crazy. I want him to want me.

And I don't want him to think I'm inexperienced.

My poem tonight is about phoning love in. Or, more specifically, about my parents. I'm the third of six poets tonight, and Caiden isn't here when Craig starts to announce me.

When I stopped by the library before class to invite him, he was helping a pretty brunette with something. They sat with their heads together at the table next to mine as he explained something to do with Shakespeare and misplaced loyalty. I waited for a few minutes and I saw him shoot me furtive glances, but I guess he couldn't break away. I left a note on his desk that just said *poetry slam tonight*, and hoped he'd get the message.

Either he didn't or didn't want to. Maybe he was just avoiding me in the library earlier. Maybe the brunette saw the note first and took it. Maybe he's with her right now.

Disappointment and doubt eat a hole in my stomach as I take the stage.

Craig snags my arm at the top of the stairs. "Was thinking we could hang out after the slam," he says in my ear, and I can smell the beer on his breath. He's only eighteen. Tino would rip his balls off if he knew he was pinching beers from cold storage.

"I might have a date," I tell him, pulling out of his grasp. "Sorry."

He bobs a slow nod as his eyes make their way to my tits. "Maybe next time."

I find my spot at the mic and take a deep breath as he backs toward the stairs, trying to center myself to read.

"There are people who we *have* to love, and others we *choose* to love, which begs the question: What, exactly, is love?"

The door of the bar opens. With the spotlight in my eyes, it's all but impossible to see anyone's face in the audience, but I pretend it's Caiden as I recite the next few lines.

And then I know it is.

I keep going, but my focus isn't on my words. It's on him as he stalks slowly toward a table in the front, close enough to the stage that the lights glow in his stormy blue eyes. He lowers himself into a chair and his attention doesn't stray, even when the waitress, Eva, comes to take his order.

Eva brings his drink just as I'm finishing. He gives her a nod as he starts to clap for me, a huge smile spreading across his strong face. The scores start to post as I make my way down the stairs to him. Mid to high nines. Pretty good scores for number three.

Caiden stands when I reach his table. "Sorry I was late. Got caught up at the library."

I try not to care that my first thought is he was fucking the brunette. Maybe he was, maybe he wasn't. It has no bearing on whether he's about to fuck *me*. I scrape my chair right up next to his, lift his drink, and down most of it in several large gulps. It burns going down and I can't stop the grimace. "Let's get out of here."

He gives me a long look, then drains the last swallow in his glass and throws a twenty on the table as he stands, pulling my chair back for me. I take his hand and we weave through the tables to the door. Once we're outside, I press up onto my tiptoes and kiss him. His arms wrap around my waist and he pulls me closer, deepening our kiss.

"That was about your family, wasn't it?" he asks when our mouths part.

I nod. "My parents, really. My brother's pretty amazing."

"You were fucking incredible. How do you do that? Come up with that powerful shit and then just put it all out there for everyone to hear?"

I shrug. "It's cheap therapy."

A smile tugs at his mouth.

"So now you know all about my supremely dysfunctional family. What's your deal?"

His smile is instantly gone. "Not much I really feel like talking about."

I scowl at him. "You're really going to shut down on me? After you just gave me props on putting all my shit out there for everyone to hear?"

"Not everyone has your courage," he says, lowering his gaze.

I search his face. There's more anger there than pain: the way the muscles of his jaw are bunched in his cheeks, the tightness around his eyes. "What if you turn it into a poem?" When he looks up with alarm in his eyes, I add, "Just for me."

He takes a deep breath and holds it for a minute before blowing it out. "I think that's harder than just telling you."

I reach for his hand, threading my fingers through his and pulling him closer. "So, just tell me."

He sandwiches my hand between both of his and watches his fingers fidget with mine. "Keri Cunningham was my first real girlfriend. She was popular, a cheerleader, beautiful; the whole package. She broke up with me a month before we graduated high school. We'd only been together for maybe four months, so in hindsight, it wasn't really that big of a thing, but she broke my heart."

He splays my hand open and starts tracing the lines of my palm, sending shivers through me. But he still won't meet my gaze.

"I'd had this grand scheme to win her back at the graduation party by fighting off all the guys who tried to hit on her, because guys were always hitting on her." His eyes lift to mine and he rolls them a little. "Thought I'd look like some kind of knight in shining armor for protecting her. Stupid, I know, but I was eighteen." His gaze lowers again. "Anyway, when she hadn't shown at the party by midnight, I finally gave up on her and went home. My mom was on the couch when I walked in. The TV was turned up full blast with one of those late-night infomercials. I thought she was just waiting up for me until I saw the mounds of tissues on the cushions around her."

He blows out a weary sigh and brings his eyes to mine, but doesn't say anything for a long time. All I can think is this girl must have died or something. I squeeze his hand to coax him along.

He takes another deep breath. "When my parents got home from my graduation, my father announced to my mother that he was in love with someone else. He was already packed and gone by the time I got home." He swallows. "Keri delivered her baby eight months later. Turns out, she broke up with me when she started fucking my forty-year-old father." He blows out a bitter laugh. "This kicker is, I never touched her. Felt guilty for even wanting to. Thought she was this sweet, perfect thing." He lets go of my hand and rubs a palm down his face. "I haven't seen or spoken to either of them since, but I heard they got married, then divorced not long after. My mother's become a bitter man-hater. She's nearly impossible to be around because—he flicks a wrist at himself—"I've got a Y chromosome, which makes me the enemy. She threw me out and my brother came with me, and that's about it. Haven't seen her in over a year." He shrugs. "And that's my fucked up family."

"Well, fuck," I say, not sure if that's an appropriate response or not, but unable to think of anything else.

"Yep. That basically sums it up."

I stretch onto my tiptoes and drop kisses along the line of his jaw. His fingers weave into the hair at the nape of my neck and he tips my mouth to meet his. His kiss is slow and his mouth grows hungrier, devouring deeper, the longer it goes.

When he finally pulls back, his eyes are a little glazed. "I'm not ready to let you go home yet."

I trace the lines of his damp lips with my finger. "Good."

"Where can we go?" His voice is rough and deepens as he asks.

A shudder sweeps through me and my inner muscles contract hard. "Walk me back to my car."

He looks around. "Where are you parked?"

"Just around the corner."

He takes my hand and we walk in silence for a block before taking a right. With each step my heart races faster. When we come to the dark lot behind the old storefronts on Main Street, mine is the only car there.

That's on purpose. The stores have all been closed for hours and this lot is always empty this time of night.

He stops next to my car and I pull him to me, kissing him hard. He twists his fingers into the hair on the back of my head and starts to devour my mouth like a starving man. I shove him back against my fender near the windshield, wrapping myself around him, and we kiss each other as if our lives depended on it.

He lifts my tank top and leans down to suck my right tit into his mouth. He rolls it under his tongue and I find out my nipple is hardwired to my groin when sparks shoot through me and my belly tingles in the aftermath. I smooth a hand over his abs to the rock-hard bulge in his jeans, then start on the button and zipper. I tug them and the snug cotton boxer briefs underneath over his hips and lower myself to my knees.

"Blaire," he warns, a throaty mix of protest and desire.

Before he can say anything else, I take him in both hands and suck him into my mouth.

An agonized groan rips out of him as he twists his fingers into my hair.

I'm afraid he's going to pull me off him, but he doesn't. I sheath my teeth behind my lips, because YouTube said that's a good way to get more pressure. He's so thick I have to open as wide as I can to suck him deep. He's not even halfway in when I gag a little. I feel his fingers tighten in my hair, pulling me back an inch. He stands perfectly still and lets me decide what happens next. I start to move my mouth over him again and it takes me another minute to find a rhythm between my hands and mouth.

I feel him, coiled tight like a wild animal ready to pounce. He holds my head gently between his hands as I move my mouth on him, never forcing me deeper that I can go without gagging. I take my mouth off him and watch his face as I explore his erection with my fingers and tongue. A drop of fluid oozes from his head and I slick the tip of my tongue along the groove there. It tastes salty.

"Christ," he groans, and his hands tighten in my hair.

An intense rush prickles under my skin at the power I have over him. I glide my tongue in a circle over the tip and he drops his head back, breaking eye contact. He pants out several breaths, then looks down at me and growls as he lifts me off the ground and throws me over the hood of the Mini. He yanks my thong to the side.

"Oh God!" I gasp when he dives under my skirt and his tongue slicks over my clit.

He sucks my clit and his tongue teases it until my whole body is a live wire. I twist my fingers into his honey waves as a long animal sound, like a cat in heat, claws its way out of me into the still night around us. I'm helpless to stop it. I roll my pelvis up to give him all of me and he eats deeper. His tongue dips inside me and I grind my hips with the rhythm of his mouth. When he sucks hard and grazes my clit with his teeth, lightning rips through my body and I arch up and scream out my orgasm.

He lifts his head from between my legs and lays his chest across my stomach, his ear against my chest. I can feel the pound of his heart, keeping time with the pulsing between my legs, where my heart seems to have lodged itself.

"I'm aching so hard to fuck you, but didn't bring protection," his breathes against my skin. "This wasn't supposed to happen."

"You could just pull out," I whisper. I want him inside me so bad that I'm pretty sure I'll die if I don't get it.

He lifts his head and looks at me, and I see the need in his storming gaze. But then he backs away and straightens my clothes. "Not here." He looks around the abandon dirt parking lot. "Not like this."

My whole body protests as he fastens his enormous erection back into his jeans.

"What if I want it here, like this?"

He steps between my knees and holds my face between his hands. "When I fuck you, it's going to be someplace where I can savor it and make it last. It's going to be somewhere I can make you come, over and over and over." He presses a kiss to my mouth. "Because I love the way you come right out loud. Just hearing you that jacked up is almost enough to get me off without you even touching me."

When he fucks me. It sounds like a promise, and it's enough that my body finally agrees to unclench.

"I love the way you *make* me come." I press my forehead against his and lower my eyes, embarrassed to confess this while I'm looking into them. "It's only ever happened with you."

He presses me back and searches my face. "You're serious?"

"You're incredible," I tell him honestly.

He smiles and kisses me, slow and deep, then lowers me off the hood and steps back and opens my door. "You're pretty fucking incredible yourself."

I slide into the seat. He closes my door and I roll the window down.

"Drive carefully," he says, kissing me through the window.

Zoey told me giving head was gross, but this time she's wrong.

Caiden's not a boy. He's a man. To know I can make him feel that way is the most intensely powerful feeling. I totally get what he said about how hearing me come could make him feel like he was going to come too. It's like I'm wired differently when we're together. Switches flip inside me and somehow we're totally connected, vibrating to the same harmonic. We amplify each other—make every sensation bigger and more intense. It's the craziest, scariest, most incredible thing I've ever felt.

And I never want it to stop.

Something fizzy, like seltzer, erupts inside me. I start the car and pull away, trying to contain it. When I turn the corner, Craig is there, smoking. He sends me a wave. I can't stop the goofy smile as I wave back.

I'm on the highway when the first kernels of my next poem start materializing in my head. *Girl Unhinged* is the title. But I'm not sure words will ever be able to capture this feeling.

CHAPTER 8

Caiden

My fingers fly over the keyboard. I'm more focused that I have been in months. Maybe it's because the mass of nervous energy that had taken up residence in my chest is gone. I can finally breathe, which means more oxygen to my brain. My final interview for the adjunct position, with the dean and department chair, is next week. It's between me and a woman from Orange County. They're scheduled to make a final decision on the same day I defend my dissertation, in four weeks.

I've managed to finish the next chapter of my dissertation ahead of schedule and my conclusion is flowing freely, pouring out of my head like Niagara Falls. I almost can't type fast enough to get one thought down before it's being drowned by the next.

My eyes keep flicking to the clock in the lit department conference room as I type. I've only got half an hour before I have to go over and beat the living shit out of Jones, then start my shift at the library.

I see Hannah in the sidelight next to the door just before it opens. She slips through and closes it behind her. "I was hoping I'd find you here." She drops her messenger bag on the floor and pulls the shade to the sidelight, blocking the view from the hall, then locks the door. "Dr. Garret is making me redo most of my research. I'm going to stab him in the fucking heart with his mother of pearl letter opener if I don't find another way to blow off this tension." She pulls off her shirt as she turns back to me.

"Hannah...I'm totally on a roll here. This is a really bad time."

"We can keep it short," she says, unhooking her bra and tossing it to the floor. "I just really need to come hard, then I'll be fine."

Fuck. My gut pulls into a hard knot. I wouldn't have made it through the last few months without her help, and she never refused it when I asked.

She shimmies out of her leggings and panties at the same time, and is lifting my shirt over my head before I can even think of what to say. The acid churning in the pit of my stomach is all the proof I need that I can't follow through with this. And I know it's because of Blaire. Just knowing the possibility of her exists is enough to ruin me for anyone else.

I grab her hand when she goes for the button of my jeans. "I really can't, Hannah. I'm sorry."

Her eyes narrow and she looks at me a long minute, then she straddles me, grinding her naked pussy against my jeans. "We're just talking five minutes so I don't fly into a murderous rampage."

I drop my head back and blow out a breath.

"I'll give you anything," she begs. "I'll type up your dissertation. Anything you want. *Please*, Caiden. I really need this."

I pull my head up and look into her eyes. What's looking back at me is something I know all too well: a combination of desperation and frustration. I skim my fingertips from her knee up her inner thigh.

"Yes," she moans and lays back against the table in front of me as I sink my fingers into her. She props onto her elbows and lolls her head back.

The image of Blaire all laid out in this same position on the hood of her Mini flashes in my mind. A sick feeling rolls through my stomach and I lift Hannah off me. "I can't do this with you anymore, Hannah."

He looks down at me, all incredulity. "You're serious."

I nod.

"You were fine with all this last week. What's changed?"

"I have." I reach for her underwear and leggings and hand them to her, then tug on my T-shirt. "I've got something going that I'm hoping might turn into something real."

She surprises me by grinning. "Are you falling in love, Caiden? Has some lucky girl finally snagged your heart?"

I hadn't thought about it in those terms. "I'm not sure yet, but I guess I want to find out."

She starts pulling her clothes on. "So, who is the fair maiden? Anyone I know?"

I gather my shit off the table and pack it into my bag. "No."

"Where did you meet her?"

My heart begins to pulse in my throat. It would feel so fucking good to have someone to talk to about this shit—get some of my frustration out in the open instead of leaving it to fester inside me, but I know it's too dangerous. "At a poetry slam."

Her eyes widen. "She's a poet?"

"One of the best I've ever heard."

"Wow. So…" She hooks her bra. "Are you dating? Or just pining?"

"Pining at the moment, but I think she's feeling it too."

"So just go for it. If you like each other, what's the hang up?"

"There's an…obstacle."

Her eyes widen. "She's got a boyfriend, doesn't she?"

I nod, even though I honestly have no fucking clue if it's true or not. I've never asked her. But I can't tell Hannah what the real issue is.

"You've got to tell her how you feel, Caiden," she says, pulling her top on. "Even if it might feel wrong while she's with someone else, you should just say it. It's the only way to know. Sometimes we use obstacles as an excuse to play it safe and not risk putting ourselves out there. I just think you'll regret it if you don't at least try, you know?"

I nod. She's totally right. I've never been so drawn to a woman. If I don't go for this and she vanishes out of my life at the end of the school year, I'll regret it forever. "Thanks, Hannah."

She pulls me into a hug. "That's what friends are for." She draws away and smiles. "Well, that and getting each other off so they don't go postal on their faculty advisors, but I'll let it slide this time."

She hikes her bag onto her shoulder and vanishes through the door, and I know what I have to do.

I'm not sure if Blaire's coming to the library tonight, and now that I know what I want to say, I can't risk missing the chance, so I abandon the deserted resource center and go to Dr. Duncan's lecture hall near the end of class. He's in the smaller of the two auditoriums in the lit building, as he only has thirty students. I slip into the back of the room and he catches my eye and sends me a salute. I nod and drop into a seat in the empty back row.

My eyes scan the room and find Blaire, seated near the front on the opposite aisle, next to a buff blond guy. She glances over her shoulder at me and smiles, then goes back to taking diligent notes.

I can't take my eyes off her, absorbing every detail so I can play it back over and over in my mind, how she crosses and uncrosses her miles of legs; the way she twists a finger into the ends of her long sable hair; how she worries her lower lip gently when she's listening; the curve of her neck when she tips her head to the side and writes.

How come I've never noticed she's a leftie?

Suddenly the room swarms, everyone rising from their seats and talking all at once, and I realize Dr. Duncan has dismissed them.

I stand and move to the aisle and see Dr. Duncan waving me down. I start down the lecture hall stairs and slow as I pass Blaire, still packing up her things.

"How's your presentation coming?" I ask, my fingers brushing her elbow.

When her nipples start to bead, I realize she's wearing a bra. I've never seen her in one before. Wasn't sure she owned any. A rush crackles under my skin when it hits me she must lose it between class and the library.

For my benefit?

"I was hoping you could look over what I have so far," she says. "Will you be in the library after this?"

"I'll walk over with you if you can wait just a minute," I say with a nod at Dr. Duncan.

"Sure," she says, and the tiniest hint of a smile sparks in her eyes.

"Mr. Brenner," Dr. Duncan says, climbing the first step to where Blaire and I are standing. "I showed Dr. Garret your dissertation drafts and he had some interesting thoughts on cross referencing the cross cultural regression with the lambda quotient from each region. I told him I'd send you in to speak with him."

I nod. "I'll set up a time."

He waves a hand at Blaire. "Have you seen Miss Leon's work so far on your friend Juan? She's got some interesting perspectives for someone so young."

I glance at her and see her hand stall midway to her messenger bag with her notebook. "We've talked some about it. She's got a gift for seeing the nuances most people miss."

"It's a talent that most of my juniors never master."

"Thank you, Professor Duncan," she says, hiking her bag. "I'm really enjoying this class."

"I'm jealous of Berkeley for stealing you away from me. I'd love to watch your insights bloom and mature over the next four years."

When I realize I'm lost in this conversation, I look at her. "You applied to grad school?"

Her panicked eyes flick to Dr. Duncan when he laughs. He claps me on the back. "She'll get here eventually, I'm certain, but our prodigy is still in high school."

The sensation is one of my veins being opened and ice water being poured directly into them. "You're in high school?" I hear myself say.

Her lips purse and there's a slight quiver in her lower one. "Yes."

CHAPTER 9

Blaire

I turn and bolt out of the lecture hall, because the betrayal in Caiden's eyes is killing me.

I should have told him the truth.

But then I wouldn't have had Friday, the most amazing night of my life. A shudder ripples under my skin at the memory of everything Caiden made me feel.

"Blaire!"

My feet stall on the sidewalk at his voice behind me. I turn and he's jogging through the dark in my direction. When he reaches me, he stops jogging but keeps moving, walking right past me. I catch up and keep pace with him.

"You told me you were a senior." His voice is low, calm, and I'm not sure what to read into it.

"I am." It's the only thing I can think to say, and it comes out hard, like I'm trying to defend it. Maybe that's exactly what I'm trying to do. I hate that it makes him think I'm less than he thought I was yesterday.

"In fucking *high school*!" he hisses, bunching a hand in his hair. "How old are you?"

"I'll be seventeen in three weeks." I hate the blood that betrays me by rising to my cheeks. I don't want to feel ashamed of wanting him.

"Jesus Christ. My kid brother is older than you." He shoves his hands into his pockets and hangs his head. "Why didn't you tell me?"

We reach my car and I turn to face him. "Because I like you, Caiden. I like you a lot. I didn't want you to think I was too young."

"But that's exactly the problem, Blaire! You *are* too young." He paces to the front of my car and stands with his back to me, rubbing a hand down his face. "Christ. This was bad enough when I thought you were a senior in *college*."

"If we both want this, why should it matter how old we are?"

He spins on me and tosses a hand at the sky. "Because I'm twenty fucking five, Blaire! Guys my age go to jail for doing what we've been doing."

I step closer. "Even if it's consensual?" One step closer and I'm right next to him. My hand brushes his thigh and I curl my fingers into the denim of his jeans. "Even if I want you so fucking much I can taste it?"

He groans and braces his hands on the hood of my car, right where my ass was when he was going down on me just three nights ago. "Yes, even then."

"That's not fair."

He shoves off the car. "Life's not fucking fair. Get used to it." He storms past me and back toward campus.

I watch until he's out of sight, then kick my tire and scream at the top of my lungs. Angry tears press behind my eyes and I swallow them back. But it's not Caiden I'm angry at. It's the world—fucking society that is trying to dictate who I can be with. I could fuck an ax murderer if he was my age and that's just fine. But I find the most incredible person I've ever met and I can't be with him because he's a few years older than me? What the fuck is that?

I kick my car again and march back toward the library. But as I get close, I see Caiden on the sidewalk near the doors, talking to Professor Duncan. All the wind leaves my sails. If he really could go to jail, is it right of me to push him there? Even if he only gets fired, I'd have ruined his life.

I really like him. If I go after him when he said no, and any of those things happen, it will all be on me. He'll resent me forever.

So I turn for my car and drive home with Arctic Monkeys full blast, the lyrics bleeding from the gaping hole in my chest.

CHAPTER 10

Caiden

It's three weeks before I see her again.

I shouldn't have left her standing there alone in the parking lot. I shouldn't have flipped my shit all over her. But up until this second, as I walk into Dr. Duncan's Nineteenth Century poetry class and her gaze finds mine like a heat seeking missile, I'd convinced myself I was in the right.

Neither of us are in the other's best interest. Whether she's scared of me after I blew up all over her, or just pissed, if it's kept her away from me, it's not a bad thing.

But Dr. Duncan is sick today and asked me to cover his class. All the students are doing at this point is prepping for their presentations, which are scheduled to start next week and run through finals. Half of the class isn't even here, opting to work on their own or maybe just blowing it off altogether.

But Blaire is.

A few students have questions on format and how to structure their presentations. Working with them serves as an adequate distraction and I'm able to avoid watching Blaire. But when the questions evaporate, I'm left sitting up here on the stool with nothing but my laptop. I pull up my dissertation PowerPoint and go over my own presentation, tweaking a few slides here and there. But with about five minutes left in class, I'm out of things to keep my mind occupied and my eyes finally slip in her direction. I get snagged in her gaze and there's nothing I can do to untangle myself. We stare at each other, both trying to see through the bullshit to what's really underneath.

"I'll be posting Dr. Duncan's presentation schedule on his webpage tonight," I say, pushing up from my stool. "For those of you who are scheduled for Monday, if you come up with any last minute questions, feel free to email me this weekend. I'll get back to you as soon as I can. Have a great weekend and good luck next week."

I drag my heels packing up, hoping Blaire will be gone by the time I'm finished, but when I look up, she's the only one left. I start up the stairs and she falls into step next to me.

I shove my hands deep into my pockets and watch the sidewalk unfold in front of me. We're halfway to the library before I finally open my mouth. "How are you about to graduate, but only sixteen?"

She flicks me a sidelong glance. "Seventeen. Today is my birthday."

Some odd aching sensation swells inside me like a tsunami. It takes me a second to recognize it's longing so intense it's physical, threatening to double me over. I give a slow nod as I breathe away the pain. "Happy birthday. But you didn't answer the question. You're young to be a senior."

"I was only in kindergarten for a two days before they promoted me to first grade because I was devouring early readers and doing simple math. I was already on the young side for my class, so..." She trails off with a shrug.

I can't stop the smile. "So, you're a child genius."

She holds my gaze. "I've always been mature for my age."

"I can believe that."

Her arm brushes mine as we walk and the contact nearly brings me to my knees. I stay focused on the five stories of concrete straight ahead. The library. Only one of my jobs here at the university.

She's only seventeen. I can't want the things I want.

We reach the library doors and I pull one open. "Are you coming in tonight?" There's an undercurrent of raw need in my voice that I despise but can't control.

She shakes her head. "Poetry slam night. They moved it up because of Memorial Day weekend and graduations and shit next Friday."

I nod as disappointment sinks heavy in my gut. "Ah, well...break a leg."

"I'll give it my best shot." She smiles and turns for the student lot.

I watch her until she's absorbed into the descending shadows, then head inside.

I can't keep my eyes off the clock. I try to distract myself with my dissertation, but all I can think about is Blaire, onstage. All I can think about is sweat glistening along the curve of her neck, and her mouth forming words that are a window into her soul.

A soul I desperately want to know intimately.

I've just decided to blow off the last half hour of my shift when a guy with floppy green hair and a skateboard under his arm crests the stairs and heads toward me. I have to restrain myself from telling him to fuck off when he drops a list on the counter in front of me.

"I need a bunch of this stuff."

"I'm on my way out," I say, shoving my laptop in my messenger bag. "Come back Monday."

He shoves a hand into his hair. "Oh, man! Seriously? Because this fucking paper is due Monday. I've got to pound it out this weekend."

"And your professor just assigned it today," I say, hoping my indifference clearly indicates I'm not feeling the need to bail him out.

"Please," he begs. "You've got to help me out here, man. I'm already on academic probation."

I take a deep breath and look at the clock. I've technically got twenty-two minutes left. I take his list off the counter and scan it. "You're never going to be able to read all of these by Monday *and* write a paper. The topic's something to do with *Bleak House*?"

He nods a little manically. "I'm supposed to write about how shit in Dickens's personal life influenced the story."

"Have you read the book?"

His face twists into a chagrinned grimace.

I take a deep breath and turn for my desk, pulling open the lowest drawer. I thumb through my personal collection of Spark Notes and find the one I'm looking for. "You're welcome," I say, handing it to him as I step around the counter. "Come on."

The kid follows me to the stacks. I pull the Dickens biography on his list that has the most information on that period of his life. I look for another that's not on his list, but might help, but find it gone. I drop the book on the table and pull it open, looking for the right section. "You're going to want to read these four chapters." I say, slipping my Spark Notes out of his hand. "And I've got some notations already in here."

We spend the next forty-five minutes pulling together a rough outline for him to follow, then I head to the desk and check him out.

"Thanks, dude!" he says with a grin as he shoves everything in his backpack.

I hike my bag onto my shoulder and hoof it toward the stairs. "Whatever. Just bring my notes back when you're done."

❖

When I push through the door into Tino's, the teenage poet who's always here is onstage. As best as I can tell coming in halfway through, his poem is about what happens when we fall short of society's expectations. But I'm only half listening, my eyes searching the room for Blaire. I find her sitting with a group of poets at a table up front.

I step up to their table and none of them notice me at first, their eyes glued to the competition on stage. But then Blaire's eyes migrate to me, as if she could feel me here.

She slips out of her seat and comes to where I'm standing. "Hi."

"Hi."

"Did I miss you?"

She nods. "First tonight."

For several beats of my hammering heart we stand here staring at each other, then she takes my hand and we walk to the door. She sees my car parked up the block and we keep walking. When we reach it, I click it open and we climb inside.

She leans toward me slowly and stops less than an inch away. Her lips are parted and her warm breath feathers my face as she stares into my eyes.

I loop my fingers behind her neck and crush her mouth in a desperate kiss. I can taste everything I need to quell this insatiable desire right there on her lips. Her fingers trickle over my chest and I can't breathe. Her touch is electric, scrambling all my synapses.

She draws away and trails a finger over the lines of my face. "Take me home with you, Caiden."

I start the engine without having to be told again, but then realize I need to check in with Chris. I text and find out he's at Taryn's tonight. He's only been home a few times since their fight, but he texts me every day so I know he's still alive.

I drive faster than I should and make the half-hour drive in twenty minutes. It's only as we're pulling up that it occurs to me I wish she didn't have to know where I live. The entire town of East Overton is a slum. I live in the ghetto of East Overton, in an apartment building full of crackheads and deadbeats.

I roll into a spot in front of the second building back from the road. There are a few gang bangers across the parking lot, one of whom I know runs the meth house in the first floor apartment under mine. One of them catcalls Blaire and I wrap my arm around her waist and pull her closer as we head up the stairs to my front door. I let us in and shut and lock the door behind us.

"Sorry about that. Not the greatest neighborhood."

"No biggie," she says absently, looking around the place.

I'm not a pig, so the apartment is fairly clean, though if I'd had any clue she would be coming home with me tonight, I would have made the bed and washed my cereal bowl. It's small, the family room only large enough for my leather couch and a coffee table. It's separated from the kitchen to the right by a short, wide island with two barstools on one end that serves as my table. The door to the left goes to my bedroom.

And that's where Blaire heads without hesitating.

I follow and watch as she sets her bag down on the corner of my queen-sized bed and divests herself of her top. There's a white lace bra underneath.

I move to her, smoothing my hands around her ribs and unhooking her bra. "Why were you never wearing a bra when you came into the library at night?"

She holds my gaze without flinching. "I wanted you to notice me. I always pulled it out my sleeve on my way from class to the library."

I blow a laugh through my nose, then step back and skim her bra straps down her arms. I bring it to my face and inhale her warm vanilla as my eyes follow the perfect contours of her full, round breasts, tipped with perfect pink nipples that harden to pebbles under my scrutiny. "There wasn't much chance I wasn't going to notice you, Blaire. You are the sexiest woman I've ever laid eyes on. From the first moment I saw you, you've been the center of my every fantasy."

She hooks her fingers under the hem of my shirt and strips it off me, then presses those incredible breasts against my chest. "I want you to fuck me so hard I forget my name, Caiden. That is *my* fantasy."

My cock was already straining against my zipper and lengthening beyond the waistband of my jeans. At her words, I have to close my eyes and breathe to keep from coming in my pants again.

Her fingers work my button as I pull my shit together, and by the time she drags my zipper down, the rush in my groin has settled to something manageable. She presses my jeans and boxers down my hips and my cock springs free, like some wild beast freed from its cage. I kick off my Vans and shuck the jeans off as she shimmies out of her skirt and panties.

And then she's on her knees in front of me. Her tongue slicks up my length from root to tip, then swirls around the head. I shudder and gently pull her away.

"If you really want to fuck, you better keep that mouth off my cock, because I'm already right on the edge of exploding."

She smiles as she stands and crawls onto the bed.

I follow her up the bed, dropping kisses along her inner thigh on the way. And when I get to that hot, sweet pussy, I dive in. She's shaved herself clean and her skin's as soft as rose petals under my mouth. She's already so fucking wet and I lap her up greedily, then eat deeper. She's got her fists in my hair and she rolls her hips and spreads wider, giving me full access to every perfect inch of her. She grinds her hips against my mouth and moans and I've got her just on the edge. But then she pulls me up her body by the hair and kisses her juices off my mouth and tongue. She reaches into her bag and comes out with a condom.

"That's not going to do it," I say looking at the Trojan in her hand. They don't make one that fits me. I reach into my drawer for the Durex XXLs I have the pharmacy order special. I sit back and roll the latex on, then look down at Blaire.

She's got the look of a woman on the edge of ecstasy, dying for someone to push her over: hooded eyes, parted lips, arched back, and fists full of sheets.

I want to be the one to take her there, but if we do this, there's no going back. I'm risking everything.

But I can't deny it. I'm falling in love with everything that she is. If there's ever been anyone worth the risk, it's Blaire.

CHAPTER 11

Blaire

The lights are on. I've only had sex in the dark before. There's something super hot about him watching as he kneels between my knees and fingers me. As if I wasn't already soaked, I feel myself gush for him. I'm shivering and my nipples are pulled painfully tight, but it's not from cold. I'm a thousand degrees under his perusal.

He withdraws the two fingers he had inside me and rubs my cum over the condom. He leans forward, supporting his weight with a hand next to my shoulder as he grabs his hard-on by the base with the other and positions himself at my opening. I feel the smooth, round head press against me and sparklers ignite in my belly as spread as wide as I can for him. This is really happening.

His ass tightens under my hands as he rolls his hips and presses harder. I feel an intense sense of stretching, but he doesn't move deeper.

"You're so tight," he says, pulling back. "Please tell me you've done this before."

The hot pulsation between my legs is suddenly rivaled by the rush of blood pulsing in my cheeks. "I have, but he was…a lot smaller."

"I don't want to hurt you." He rolls on his back and pulls me to straddle him. "We'll start here. You're in control this way. If it hurts, we'll stop."

I'm not going to stop. No matter what.

He uses his fingers to spread my lips open. I take his dick in my hand and guide him to my opening. I hold him there as I lower myself slowly down. He's holding his breath and lying perfectly still, waiting for me to let him in. He's not far inside when I feel a sudden sharp sting. I whimper.

"Blaire?" he asks, concern threading with the throaty lust in his tone as he grasps my hips and lifts me off him.

"I'm okay," I say, prying his fingers loose and pressing myself lower. I feel every inch of him, one at a time, as he sinks through my core and touches my soul. Once my ass is resting on his thighs I wait, feeling him inside me; how he stretches me. Fills me.

He holds still as I adjust to his firm pressure inside. "There's not even a fucking word that describes this feeling, Blaire," he groans.

As I start to gently rock my hips, he sucks his thumb then rubs it over my clit. He coordinates the circles of his thumb to the grinding of my hips, and I feel that hot electrical ache swell inside me.

"Don't hold back," I tell him when I realize he's laying still, giving me total control. "You're not going to hurt me. I want it harder."

Caiden starts to move with me, grasping my hip and rolling his pelvis under mine, and I feel him even deeper. He increases the pressure of his thumb on my clit and I gasp.

"Okay?" he asks.

"Fuck, yes," I moan, quickening my movements. "Harder."

He hooks his knee over my legs and in one deft move has me on my back. I bring my knees up as high as I can and he drives himself into me to the hilt. I cry out as sparks skitter under my skin and hot pressure builds inside me like a volcano. With each thrust, my cries become louder and more animal, a sharp "Ah!" which turns into one long mewl when I lose all control. My spine arches and my mouth freezes in a silent scream as the volcano erupts and warmth explodes through my belly. My body turns suddenly liquid. Stars flash in my eyes.

I can't move. I can barely breathe.

Caiden gives two more hard thrusts, then growls out loud and collapses on top of me. I feel his dick pulsing inside me and it sends shivers up my spine.

"I love your dick," I pant into his chest before I think better of it.

He chuckles. "Watch out. You're going to give it a big head."

I squeeze his ass cheeks, pulling him tighter against me. "I *want* your dick to have a big head so you can fuck me again."

He presses up and lifts his weight off of me, looking down into my eyes. "Be careful. You're bound to get your wish."

I run a hand over my boob and pluck at my nipple. "Good."

"Fuck me," he groans, then pulls out of me.

I sit up and watch him peel the condom off.

There's concern in his eyes when they meet mine again. "There's some blood here. Are you sure you're okay?"

I glance down at the sheets and find them clean. "Never better."

As I say it, my stomach rumbles.

He's just reaching for another condom and a smile ticks up one side of his mouth. He scoops me off the mattress and carries me to the kitchen. "I need to feed you first."

He sets my naked ass on the island with the barstools and opens the fridge, peering in.

"Leftover pepperoni pizza?" he asks, glancing over his shoulder at me. When I shake my head he pulls a Chinese takeout box off the shelf and opens it. "Chicken chow mein?"

"No thanks."

He puts it back and yanks open the freezer. "Chocolate ice cream?"

I smile. "Yes, please."

He grabs the container and pulls a spoon from the drawer next to the sink on his way back to me. He dips the spoon into the container and holds a large bite of ice cream to my mouth. I open and suck some off the end.

He eats the rest in one bite then dips the spoon into the container again. "We're going to have to be careful at school," he says, holding another bite up for me.

"I know." I suck some off the spoon and a dribble of chocolate escapes my mouth and falls on my chest.

He licks it off, then dips his finger into the container and finger paints more ice cream onto my nipples, before licking me again. He carves out another large bite and holds it to my mouth.

I take some off the spoon and brush it down his chest, then lick it off.

He drops his head back and groans.

I paint more ice cream onto his thickening dick, then slide off the counter and lick him. He stiffens to a hard rod as I suck him deeper, his fingers twisting into my hair.

"Christ, Blaire," he says, lifting me by the shoulders. "You never run out of ways to blow my fucking mind."

He turns me and I brace my elbows on the counter and arch my back as he wedges himself between my legs. This time, when he takes me from behind, he glides right into my wet heat like a knife through melting butter. He starts slow, but when I start rocking my weight back as he thrusts, he takes my cue and grasps my hips, pounding himself into me to the hilt.

He's not wearing protection, and there's a second that I think about saying something, but he reaches around and finds my clit, and I forget everything but what he's making me feel. His fingertips stroke to the rhythm of our slapping skin, faster and deeper each time he drives himself into me, and it's only seconds later that I'm screaming. He goes longer, and the sensation in my belly is firecrackers when you light the pack. Pop! Pop! Pop! One after the other. I come at least five times in thirty seconds and it feels like my whole body seizes.

I sag against the counter when my legs refuse to hold me anymore. He pulls out and lifts me into his arms, carrying me back to his bed. He lays me across it and retrieves a condom, sheathing his rock-hard dick.

I scoot over to make room as he climbs in next to me, then pull him on top of me. "Fuck me more," I whisper.

He gazes down at me for several beats of my racing heart, then gives me what I want. We kiss and fuck and it's slow and intense and lazy and crazy and even though he's not going hard, it reaches deeper into me than anything ever has, pulling at my heart and drawing emotions out of it that I never knew were there.

He kisses my temple and that's when I realize I'm crying.

"I've got you," he whispers in my ear.

I come twice more before he does, but I don't scream. It feels more like doors of a dusty attic being blown open by the first breeze of spring, just a whoosh through my body that leaves everything clean and new.

And that's when I realize.

I'm falling in love with Caiden.

"Can you stay?" he asks softly into my hair. "I can't imagine anything that could make this better except waking up in the morning with you here."

"Yeah, I can stay." There have been a few times I've stayed at Zoey's after we'd been out partying, and Mom and Dad never even missed me.

Caiden gets up and goes to the bathroom. He's back a few minutes later. I slide over and he climbs into the bed next to me. We kiss and touch and I forget the world and just live in Caiden. I wrap myself around him and he tangles his legs into mine.

And that's exactly where we are when I wake up to the pink of morning light.

A new day. A new life.

One where someone wants me for more than just a few minutes. One where the person whose life I'm tangled into *chose* to be here.

CHAPTER 12

Caiden

Blaire's eyes are alight when she finds me in the library after her presentation. Her whole face glows the same way it does when she's performing her poetry at Tino's. She splays her hands on the counter and leans toward me. "Kiss me," she whispers.

I flash a glance at the room to double check that we're alone and, Christ, do I want to do as I'm told. I feel her draw like a magnet. But instead I pull a shaky breath. "How was your presentation?"

"Amazing." A wicked smile curves her lips. "We can celebrate properly when you're through here."

The way I'm feeling, like I'm going to break into fucking song or something at any second, I wish with every fiber of my being Friday had been her eighteenth instead of her seventeenth. I don't want to hide what we have. I want to take her places. I want to spend all my time with her, both in bed and out of it. "Tell me about all this 'amazing,'" I say to keep us in the present because, looking into her eyes, I feel myself being pulled back to the bliss of waking with her in my arms Saturday morning.

A grin breaks over her face. "I wrote it as a poem and slammed it. It was epic."

I laugh and give my head a shake. "You seriously did, didn't you?" She never stops surprising me.

"You bet your sweet ass."

At her mention of my ass, I can't stop myself from taking another look around the room to be sure it's empty. "I'm sure that was a first for Dr. Duncan. What did he say?"

Her grin widens. "That it was brilliant and the other students should take note of my ingenuity."

I get lost in her darkening whiskey eyes. "You're fucking incredible."

"I am," she says, and God, I want to kiss her.

Instead, I back away a step. "So, you're done with classes?"

She gives me a funny look. "I've got three more weeks before graduation."

Right. I'm choosing not to think about the fact she's still in high school. "But you're done here at Sierra. Berkeley bound next term."

As I say it, a dark surge of jealousy rises in my chest and rakes talons across the deepest layers of my heart. Her smile fades as she nods and I know she heard it in my voice.

I turn and pull a file off my desk. It isn't even mine—
something the guy who had the shift before me left—but
I pretend to be suddenly gripped by it. "You'll be moving
on to smarter graduate assistants, then."

It's only after it's out of my mouth that I realize how
cruel it sounded.

"Why would you even say that?" she asks before I
can think of how to backpedal. The raw wound in her
voice nearly kills me.

I haul a deep breath to settle the riot in my head, then
lower the file, bringing my focus back to Blaire. As the
chaos inside settles, I find the words that I really meant to
say. "Because, this isn't all there is for you, Blaire. I can
feel it. This is all just an insignificant pit stop on your
road to something so much bigger."

She gives a quick look around the empty resource
center before taking my hand and towing me past the
tables and into the stacks. We're three rows deep when
she turns the corner and stops. "There's nothing
insignificant about you, Caiden." Color rises to her face,
but she doesn't lower her gaze. "You are everything. I'm
in love with you."

I hang my head and lean back against the stacks for
balance as the electric rush that crashes through my body
threatens to take me to my knees. She steps closer,
pressing her body against mine.

My arms close around her.

We kiss. Then we kiss deeper. In my desperation to climb right into this incredible woman, I find myself lifting her off the ground.

She wraps her legs around my waist, hiking her skirt up to her hips in the process.

I turn us so her back is against the shelves and crush her between the books and my body, needing the full measure of her pressed against every inch of me. She kisses me so desperately I feel my soul rise up and blend with hers.

Her hand slips between us, working my fly. I make room for her, and when she has my cock out, I yank her underwear aside and bury myself inside her wet heat.

She digs her heels into my ass and I thrust against her, over and over, driving myself into her as deeply as humanly possible, trying to root myself there. I smother her cries and moans with my mouth, desperate not to let even that tiny bit of her escape me. I want all of her. She owns me and everything she is, is mine.

But the next second, she's ripped out of my arms.

My heart thuds to a stop as my eyes snap to where Dr. Duncan clutches her in front of him tightly by both upper arms.

"What in the world...?" he asks, staring, wide-eyed over Blaire's shoulder at my raging erection.

I pull myself together enough to fasten my jeans as I glance down at Blaire. Her face is ashen and her eyes glisten with moisture in the dim lighting as she smooths down her skirt.

The earth tilts, throwing me off balance. This wasn't supposed to happen.

"I'm sorry," I hear myself say, but I'm not sure who I'm apologizing to and for what. Getting caught? The fact I let it go this far in the first place? Or for not standing up and defending it now?

"I want you off the premises, Mr. Brenner," Dr. Duncan growls. "*Now*, before I call security."

He manhandles Blaire around the corner of the stacks toward the elevator.

When the floor has stopped pitching under my feet and I have my bearings, I turn the corner and stagger to the tables. I brace my hands on the back of a chair as the elevator doors slide shut. Just before she vanishes from sight, Blaire catches my gaze, and I see something in her eyes that nearly kills me.

Regret.

CHAPTER 13

Blaire

"I can't even..." Professor Duncan trails off and shakes his head. "I don't have words right now. There is no excuse for Mr. Brenner's—" His face pulls into a mask of disgust so red I'm afraid he's about to blow a blood vessel. "—behavior," he finishes after a second. "He..." He trails off again and lowers his gaze. "I will help you in any way I can. There is a crisis counselor on staff here at Sierra I think you should speak with."

"I'm fine," I say, but it's weak. I'm not fine.

Everything Caiden was worried about just happened.

Guys my age go to jail for doing what we've been doing.

What if I've brought his every fear to fruition?

When Professor Duncan meets my gaze again, it's clear he doesn't believe me.

He takes off his glasses and rubs his eyes. "I feel responsible. I placed my trust in Mr. Brenner...put him in a position to..." He drops back in his chair. "I had no idea he was a pedophile."

At the word, my heart lurches. "He's not!"

His eyes lift to mine and go sickeningly sympathetic; it's the type of sympathy reserved for the mentally challenged or the very young when they've done something horribly embarrassing but aren't capable of understanding they should be embarrassed. "I know this has been traumatic for you, Blaire. I'll take you home and help you speak with your parents about it."

I bolt out of my chair. "God, no!"

Terror pumps rivers of adrenaline through my racing mind. This is really happening. Caiden is going to lose his job...maybe go to jail. It's all happening because I didn't leave him alone when he asked me to.

I could have walked out of class Friday night instead of waiting for him. He wouldn't have come to the slam. He wouldn't have taken me home.

He wouldn't have taken me home.

And the single most intense experience of my life would never have happened. It's the most selfish thought I've ever had, but that was the most real night of my life.

"There's nothing for you to be ashamed of," he says, standing from his chair, as if he thinks it's impolite for him to sit while I'm standing. "You are a child. You were taken advantage of by someone in a position of authority. None of this is your fault."

But it's all my fault. I'm the one who pulled my bra out my sleeve every evening between class and seeing Caiden in the library. I'm the one who made the first move and kissed him. My hand was in his pants before his was ever in mine. But telling that to Professor Duncan isn't going to help.

"Caiden didn't do anything wrong."

His eyes widen. "Miss Leon," he says, his tone turning from sympathy to admonition. "Even if he was not my graduate student, had I found *any* student in the position I found him in, I would have had him removed from campus. The fact that he was your mentor only makes the offense that much more egregious." He picks up his phone. "Let me at least call your parents to come for you. This has been a traumatic experience. I don't believe you should be driving home alone."

"I'm fine to get home on my own. My car is in the student lot. And I'll talk to my mother when I get there."

He sets his desk phone down and pulls his cell off the clip on his belt. "What is your phone number? I want to call after you've had the discussion with your family."

I give him my cell number because there's no way I want him talking to my parents without having to go through me first. He types it into his phone then lifts his desk phone again.

"I need a security escort for a student from Benton Hall to the student parking lot. And then I need you to confirm that Caiden Brenner is out of the resource center on the fifth floor of the library and off the university grounds."

He stands and walks with me to the front of the building. "I'm so sorry for my role in this, Blaire. I can't undo what happened, but rest assured, I'll do everything in my power to make this right for you. I'm so sorry."

"I'm really okay," I say, and try harder to sound like I mean it. "He didn't *make* me do anything."

Sympathy slips over his features again and I want to slap it off his face. "Talk to your family. When you're ready, I will give you the name of our counselor."

A uniformed security guard pulls in front of the building in a golf cart and Professor Duncan nods to him as I descend the stairs to the sidewalk without another word. He doesn't speak and neither do I, and when I get home, I give Mom a wave on my way past the family room and go straight to bed.

In the dark of the room, cocooned under the sheets, I finally let myself feel everything I've been struggling to keep at bay. I feel the heavy dread in Caiden's eyes when he realized we'd been caught. The weight of it sinks me halfway through the mattress. I feel Professor Duncan's sympathy and the security guard's curiosity. I feel paralyzing shock tighten my chest and force the air from my lungs. I feel the press of cold fear grip me first by the stomach, making me feel sick, then by the throat. And last, I feel aching emptiness. Because, wherever I go from here, it's going to be without Caiden.

When my phone vibrates with Professor Duncan's call, I don't answer.

I've spent every minute of the two days since Professor Duncan caught us in the library either on the phone with Caiden, or waiting for the other shoe to drop. When I'm called to the school office in the middle of second period AP calculus, I know it has.

Principal Elbridge meets me outside her office, and from the practiced sympathy ingrained into her features, I know she knows.

"Blaire," she says, laying a hand between my shoulder blades and guiding me to her closed door, garnering a curious look from the administrative assistant at the reception desk as we pass through the outer office. "I'm sorry to pull you out of class. If it wasn't of the utmost importance, I wouldn't have. There is someone who needs to speak with you in my office."

She opens the door into the cluttered space and a woman in a green blouse and black slacks stands from the chair next to Principal Elbridge's desk.

"Blaire Leon?" she asks.

I nod as Principle Elbridge nudges me the rest of the way through the door so she can close it.

The woman is Hispanic and there's none of the sympathy I've seen in Professor Duncan and Principal Elbridge's eyes in her big dark ones. For a second I think maybe I'm here for some other reason. Until she says, "I'm Detective Diaz. I have a few questions for you." She looks at the principal. "Can we have your office for a moment?"

Principal Elbridge blinks, confused. "I don't think—"

"I'm sure Blaire appreciates your concern," she interrupts, "but I think her interests are best served if we chat alone."

Her eyes narrow at the woman before she turns her attention to me. "Blaire? Are you comfortable with this?"

I feel my armor go up, even though Detective Diaz doesn't look at me like I'm clueless. "Yeah."

"I will be just outside the door," she says. "You can walk out at any point."

"I'll be fine."

She gives me a long look, then slips out the door.

"Would you like to sit?" the detective asks.

Blood thunders in my ears as I move to one of the chairs near the desk and sit.

She lowers herself into the seat next to me. "Let me cut right to the chase, Blaire. We've received a report of sexual contact between you and one of the teaching staff at Sierra State."

Fuck. It could only have been Professor Duncan.

I shake my head. "I don't know what you're talking about."

Her gaze turns more assessing, scouring my face. "I'm just trying to get to the truth here, Blaire. A police report was filed. We're legally bound to investigate any report such as this involving a minor."

There's a rush of adrenaline to my bloodstream when I see Caiden's way out. If I deny it, it's Professor Duncan's word against mine. "Your report is wrong."

"So, you deny having sexual intercourse with Caiden Brenner in the Sierra State library?"

"We're just friends. That's all." I hardly hear my words through the rush of blood in my ears.

She gives me a slow nod and pulls a small spiral notebook out from a black bag on the corner of Principal Elbridge's desk. "You know," she says without lifting her eyes from what she's writing, "I was seventeen once too. I understand you can't always control who you have feelings for." She lowers her notebook and her eyes raise to mine. "All I really want is to know that you're okay."

There's no judgment in her statement. I look at her more closely. She's younger than my parents, maybe in her late thirties. She doesn't come across as a hard-ass cop, but more like someone who really wants to help. I picture myself telling her the truth. She seems like someone who wouldn't flip out and overreact. She might *get* Caiden and me. But just as I'm opening my mouth I realize that if I say it, I can never take it back. If I'm wrong about her, she'll send Caiden to jail.

"He's just a friend."

She looks down at the notebook. "He's a teaching assistant for one of your classes?"

I nod.

"Have you ever done anything together outside of school?"

I think about the poetry slams he's been to. It wouldn't be too hard for her to find out we've been seen together. But no one there would have seen us kiss, or even touch, really, except for the shoulder rub that Eva saw me give him the first time he came, back in January. "He's into poetry, so he's come to a few of my poetry slams. Nothing else."

She gives me a slow nod. "Is there anything else you think I should know, Blaire?"

I shrug, trying to come off casual. "No."

The passing bell rings and she stands. "All right, then, I'll let you get back to class."

I gain my feet and am surprised to find my legs a little unsteady.

She holds out a card to me. "If there's anything I can do for you, or you think of anything else you want to tell me that might help with the investigation, just give me a call."

My stomach cramps. That doesn't sound like she's letting it drop. "Nothing happened." I say, taking it from her hand.

She nods. "Thanks for your time."

I walk quickly through the outer office toward the bustling hall. Principal Elbridge is behind the counter on the phone. I hear her call after me but I don't slow down. I keep my head down and weave my way through the throng and out the front doors. Once outside, it's suddenly quiet. I slow down and focus on breathing as I move toward the student lot, because my fingers and toes are starting to tingle.

"Yo! Bitch!" I hear from behind me just as I clear the gate into the lot.

Shit. Zoey. I slow and turn as she comes jogging up behind me.

"Jessica said you got called out of class," she pants as she catches up. "What up?"

I start heading to my car. "Just something to do with my transcript for Berkeley."

Even though she can barely breathe after her sixty foot dash, she goes for a cigarette in her bag. "So why are we blowing out of school? You never cut class."

"*We* aren't doing anything," I say, clicking my lock. "I don't feel great. I'm going home."

She flicks her lighter and takes a deep drag. "How am I supposed to get home?"

"You have other friends, Zoe," I say, dropping into my seat. "Worst case, Kevin can piggyback you."

She pulls a face. "I spread my legs around him, his mind will head in an entirely different direction."

I close my door and roll down my window. "He worships the ground you walk on."

"So…you're really just going home to puke?" she asks.

I shrug. "Sorry."

She bangs her palm on the roof. "Text me if you're not coming to school tomorrow. I'll find another ride."

I nod and start the car. I peal onto the road and as I pass the faculty lot, I see Principal Elbridge standing out front next to a black sedan with Detective Diaz. They both look up as I pass and I turn my head quickly. But I know I'm busted.

I hit the gas and don't stop until I'm parked in front of Caiden's building.

CHAPTER 14

Caiden

Blaire left my house Saturday morning with my cell number and my heart.

And then everything went to hell.

I spent most of last night and the night before on the phone with her, trying to talk her down. She's terrified she's ruined my life. I lied and told her everything was going to be okay.

I watched the sun rise hours ago, but I'm still in bed contemplating my sorry life when frantic pounding at my front door jolts me upright. I glance at the clock and find it's after ten. My heart hammers as I climb out of bed and go to the window, expecting flashing police lights. What I see instead is Blaire's shiny Mini.

I tug on a T-shirt and jeans and race to the door, throwing it open. The next second she's in my arms.

I've asked her to stay away, as much for her as for me, but now everything I need is right here in my arms.

And it's killing me. I kick the door shut and hold her close when I realize she's crying.

"Hey," I say, stroking her hair. "Everything's going to be okay."

"No it's not," she says into my shirt. She sniffles and lifts her damp face. "A detective was at school this morning. Professor Duncan filed a police report. I told her we were just friends and the report was wrong, but..." She presses her face against my shoulder. "I don't think she believed me."

There's a moment that all the blood leaves my head and the room goes gray. This is it. It's happening. "You should tell them the truth."

She pulls out of my shirt and her eyes snap to mine. "You said they could send you to jail."

"I don't want you to lie for me, Blaire. You didn't do anything wrong."

At my words, the shock in her expression is exchanged for indignation. "Neither did you!"

"And if we're up front with them, they might believe that. It's our best chance."

"No," she says with an adamant shake of her head. "It's Professor Duncan's word against ours. They can't prove anything if we deny it."

I take a deep breath and guide her to the couch. We sink into it and she settles into my side. Every cell in my body hums with the contact. How can something so wrong it will send me to prison feel so right? "Did you mean what you said in the library?"

Those incredible whiskey eyes meet mine, and in them I see a future I want more desperately than any degree, any career. "You should know by now I don't waste words. I mean *everything* I say."

I press my face into her hair and breathe in her warm vanilla. "How did we get so deep so fast?"

"Didn't Dr. Seuss say something like, 'You'll know when you're in love when you can't fall asleep because reality is finally better than your dreams.'?"

Despite our current circumstances, a smile pulls at my mouth. "I think so."

"And Richard Bach said, 'A soulmate is someone who has locks that fit our keys, and keys to fit our locks.'"

"That's not from *Jonathan Livingston Seagull*."

"*The Bridge Across Forever*."

"Ah. Makes much more sense."

"I have so many locks, Caiden," she says, her voice hitching on my name. "But you fit them all."

I pull her closer as my heart shatters.

She settles deeper into my side. "Did you know only ten states set the legal age of consent at eighteen? In thirty two states it's sixteen."

"So we had the bad luck to live in the wrong place." I press my lips to the crown of her head and stroke her hair. I let myself have this for right now, not really knowing if it's right or wrong and not really caring just at this moment.

"What are we going to do?" she says, her voice little more than breath against my neck.

I peel her gently back and look into those mesmerizing eyes. "Whatever we have to."

She leans toward me, but just as our lips touch, there's a knock.

Both our faces turn toward the door and my dread is mirrored in her eyes.

"You should go into the bedroom," I say, unwrapping myself from her and standing.

She stares at me a moment longer then does as I asked. When she's out of sight, I move to the door and look through the peephole. On my landing is a Hispanic woman in a green blouse. I finger comb my hair and pull open the door.

"Caiden Brenner?" she asks.

My heart is hammering in my chest and I fight to keep the adrenaline out of my voice. "Yes."

"I'm Detective Diaz. I wondered if I might have a word with you about Blaire Leon?"

I nod and swing the door wider for her to pass.

She steps inside and takes a second to scan the room. "Is it okay if I sit?" she asks, gesturing to the couch.

"Sure." We move that direction and I shake off some of my daze. "Can I get you something to drink?"

"No, thank you," she says, lowering herself into the end of the couch and placing her bag on the floor next to her feet. "This should only take a few minutes."

I take the seat on the opposite end.

She pulls a pen and small scratch pad from her bag and angles herself toward me. "I have a rather delicate situation, Mr. Brenner. Your faculty advisor at Sierra State has filed a very explicit report with the police describing sexual activity between you and an underage student from his class in the library on Monday evening. I'd like you to tell me what happened."

Blaire just told her it wasn't true. If I say anything else before she has a chance to recant, I'm calling her out as a liar. But I'm not as convinced as Blaire that they'll dismiss Dr. Duncan's statement if we deny it. If I back Blaire's lie and we're discovered, it will look that much more sordid.

"I'd like you to remember that you're the adult in this scenario, Mr. Brenner," she says, reading my hesitation. "Miss Leon is seventeen. I know in reality she's not exactly a child, but in the eyes of the law, she needs to be protected if protection is in order. I just need to know she's okay."

I can feel Blaire in the next room and I know she's hanging on every word. If I don't play along, she's likely to burst out here and blow this whole thing up.

"Blaire Leon is an incredible person. She's passionate and talented and so full of spirit that sometimes I get lost in it. But Dr. Duncan was mistaken in what he thought he saw."

"So you're saying you've never had sexual intercourse with Blaire Leon?"

I shake my head. "No."

"Well, then, I'm sorry to have bothered you." She stands. "I appreciate your time, Mr. Brenner."

I see her to the door.

As she steps through, she pulls a card out of her bag. "Just in case you think of anything else."

I take it and close the door as she starts down the stairs. I watch through the peephole as she lays her hand on the hood of Blaire's Mini, parked just outside, then glances back at my door.

And I know I'm screwed.

Blaire bounces out of the bedroom, all smiles. "It's going to be okay."

I don't contradict her, because the way her face looks right now, glowing and wide open, makes me feel so full inside I could live off of the sensation forever. I fold her tightly into my arms and kiss her forehead. "You need to go back to school."

Her fingers find the hem of my T-shirt and tug. "I had something else in mind."

I gently grasp her wrist and bring the backs of her fingers to my mouth, brushing her knuckles across my lips. "I'm already responsible for besmirching your honor. I'm not going to be responsible for your delinquency too."

She shakes her head as some of the glow vanishes from her face. "This is what they don't see. If I'd made that proposition to any guy in my high school class, he'd be towing me out the door for a quickie in his car. But this is wrong," she says with a wave of her hand between us. "Even though you actually give a shit about me."

I kiss her slowly then draw back. "I more than 'give a shit' about you, Blaire."

She sinks into my chest and I hold her for a long time. Finally, I pry her away. "You really need to go back to class."

Her fingertips find my face and she trails them over my jaw line. "I love you."

The unabashed love in her gaze stalls my heart and steals my breath. "Those words don't feel like enough."

"Then I'll think of better ones," she says, stretching up and pressing her mouth to mine.

Our bodies are better at conveying exactly how we feel and it's minutes later we finally part.

"You need to go now, before I change my mind," I say.

One of her perfect black brows arches and a wicked smile tugs at her mouth. "What if I want you to change your mind?"

The thought that this might be my last chance to be with her hits me like a wrecking ball. The temptation to tow her into the bedroom and spend the rest of the day demonstrating just how much I love her is overpowering. I teeter on the precipice for a long moment before reaching for the door handle. *I'd like you to remember that you're the adult in this scenario, Mr. Brenner.* Time to act like one. "Call me when you're done at school."

She presses up onto her toes. "They're not going to win," she whispers, then kisses me. "They can't keep us apart."

I pull open the door and she steps through, but when she glances back at me from her car, the same way Detective Diaz did, I know she's wrong.

CHAPTER 15

Blaire

Caiden says it too risky to see each other while we're being investigated, and just yesterday, he told me we shouldn't talk on the phone either. He's shutting me out and I don't know what to do about it.

But I've done as he asks, because I'm starting to worry that I screwed this up. Gloria called me two days ago and said Detective Diaz was questioning people from Tino's. I don't think anyone there saw us doing anything but talking.

I don't think.

But what if they did? I've played everything over in my head, and there was a kiss on the sidewalk someone might have seen.

My window is open and the soft sun of an early-June morning slants across my bed. It feels good on my skin. I use the sensation to ground me in this moment and keep my thoughts from drifting.

Everything is going to be fine. No one saw anything.

Someone is knocking around in the kitchen and I know it has to be Mom. Dad is gone for the weekend to some convention in San Diego, and even though Marcus just got home from L.A. last night, there's no way he's up at nine on a Saturday morning.

I'm hunched over my AP history book. With graduation only a few weeks away, most everyone in my class has checked out, including Zoey, even though she's only a junior. Most teachers have given up and stopped assigning homework. But not mine. My acceptance to Berkeley is provisional. I can't get a B in this class.

The third time through the reading, it finally starts to make sense, words and paragraphs coming together in fully formed concepts that I can grasp, and when there's a knock at my bedroom door, I realize that I've gone nearly a full hour without obsessing over Caiden.

"Yeah?" I say.

Mom cracks open my door. My senses go on high alert when I see her ashen complexion and the concern lining her face. "Blaire, honey, there's someone here to speak to you. Can you come downstairs?"

"Um..." I look down at my T-shirt. "Okay. Just give me a sec."

She nods and closes the door. I hear her feet on the stairs, then voices. She's talking to a woman. How did I not hear the door?

I go to the window and look out at the street. Parked behind my Mini at the curb is the black sedan I saw at the high school. The urge to climb out the window is overwhelming, but it's a two-story drop with no handy trellis or tree. And disappearing will only make us look guiltier.

I yank on the shorts from the floor near my bed and trudge downstairs. Detective Diaz is sitting on the sofa, sipping a cup of coffee.

She sets her coffee down and stands when she sees me. "Blaire," she says.

Mom comes in from the kitchen and we all sit.

"I may have overstepped," Detective Diaz says. "I didn't realize you hadn't discussed your situation with Caiden Brenner with your family."

I shoot a panicked glance at Mom. She looks confused...or really more blindsided, but she won't meet my eyes. "I told you, there is no 'situation.'"

She looks at me for a long moment, then turns to my mother. "I wonder if I can have a moment alone with Blaire."

Mom nods and rises from her seat. Finally her eyes find mine. "I'll be in the bedroom...if you need me."

I almost laugh out loud at the notion of her "being there for me," but something in her expression stops me. Under her shock is something deeper. Something maternal. I feel my heart bunch.

She looks back from the door, once again relaying some message I'm not quite grasping with her eyes, then slips into her room.

Once the door closes behind her, Detective Diaz reaches into her bag on the floor at her feet and pulls out an iPad. "I need you to see something." She taps on it a few times then turns it for me to see. A supernova explodes in my chest as a video of me on the hood of the Mini plays. The clip is dark and grainy, but there's no mistaking what Caiden is doing to me, his head between my legs and his fingers digging into my ass as I moan out sounds that aren't even human.

Gloria said they were questioning people from Tino's. But who would have seen this? Who would have recorded it?

"Where did you get this?" I hear myself say.

"It doesn't matter," she says in the same calm voice that I'm just starting to realize is her way of lulling a person into a false sense of security. "I have no choice but to arrest him. I just wanted you to be prepared."

Panic kicks in my stomach. "I don't want to press charges."

She shakes her head. "This is a criminal case, Blaire. It's not up to you or me what happens to Caiden now."

"You can't do this!" I bolt off the sofa. "I don't want this!"

"Blaire," the detective says, holding up her hands to show she's no threat. "I just need to know the truth so I can help you."

"I don't need help."

Mom is back. "I think you should leave," she says to Detective Diaz.

"Your daughter wasn't honest with me when I first asked her about Caiden Brenner," she says. "I'm just trying to get to the truth."

Mom looks at me and now that the shock is wearing thinner, I can see the fierceness in her eyes. She turns her sharp gaze back to the detective. "The *truth* is, she doesn't want to press charges. I don't understand why she needs to be dragged through this."

"If she and Mr. Brenner had been up front about their relationship from the beginning, there's a chance it wouldn't have come to this."

I want to scream at her that we're in love, but I know, in her eyes, that would only make me look more the naïve, manipulated little girl.

Mom brushes past us to the door and opens it. "You need to go."

Detective Diaz splits a glance between us, then nods. "You may hear from the court or Mr. Brenner's attorney, depending on how he pleads."

She holds out her hand but Mom doesn't shake it. She takes the hint and turns for her car.

There's a long minute where Mom and I just stare at each other, before she closes the distance between us and pulls me into her arms. "Are you okay?"

"No."

"What can I do?" she asks.

I drop my head onto her shoulder, surprised at how much just this calms the storm in my mind. "I don't think there's anything anyone can do."

"About what?"

We both turn toward Marcus's voice on the stairs.

He rubs the sleep out of his eyes as he reaches the bottom. "Who were you yelling at?"

Mom looks at me and I nod. Marcus isn't going to like this, but better he hears it from me.

"I've been...seeing someone."

"And...?" he says, dropping into the sofa.

I sit next to him and Mom takes the armchair. "He's older."

Marcus's face hardens. "How much older?"

"Twenty-five."

His jaw flexes as his eyes flash. "What did he do?"

I shake my head. "Nothing. He didn't do anything wrong."

"Did he touch you?" Marcus grinds out through clenched teeth.

"I love him, Marcus." I lay a hand on his arm. "He didn't do anything to me that I didn't ask him to."

"So, what's happening? Who was here?"

"He's being arrested," Mom chimes in.

Marcus stands, then sits, then stands again. He looks at me and nods. "Good." He paces to the kitchen, then back. "Good."

"It's not good!" I stand and stare him in the eye. "He didn't do anything wrong."

He laughs under his breath. "There's something seriously sick about a twenty-fucking-five-year-old who thinks screwing around with a sixteen-year-old is okay."

"I'm seventeen," I say, "and age doesn't mean shit! You don't get to choose who you love, Marcus!"

He paces the room again, his hand fisted into his hair, then grabs his keys from the counter and storms out the front door.

I stare after him until I hear the roar of his engine and the peal of tires out front.

Mom has me in her arms again, and it feels both foreign and familiar. But I'm so thankful for at least one ally—in the place I least expected to find one—that I sink into her and let the tears I've been denying myself fall.

But Detective Diaz's words in my head stop me mid-sob. *I have no choice but to arrest him.*

I tear out of Mom's grasp and bolt up the stairs to my room. I grab my phone and dial. I'm afraid he's not going to pick up. When he does, I let out the breath I was holding.

CHAPTER 16

Caiden

"They're coming for you, Caiden!"

My heart turns to molten lead and sinks into the depths of hell at Blaire's words through the phone.

"It's okay," I say automatically. I've been preparing for this since Detective Diaz left here three days ago.

"It's not okay! You need to get away from here. Run!"

I haul a deep breath and try to find myself inside my shell of a body. "I can't run, Blaire."

"You have to. She said I can't stop it…that it's up to the courts now. She's coming to arrest you."

In my alternate reality, I was supposed to be defending my dissertation tomorrow afternoon and waiting to hear if I'd landed the adjunct faculty gig. But that all changed in a heartbeat. I'm quite aware that the repercussions here are far greater than just the job I'm never going to get now. I'm royally and thoroughly fucked.

I pinch the phone between my shoulder and ear and yank my jeans on. "I need you to listen to me, Blaire. You need to cooperate with the police." I swallow. "And I need you to stop trying to contact me."

Not for me. I'm done caring about me. I've lost everything that matters—Blaire, my degree, my career, my self-respect. Blaire told me she loves me, but I'm not allowed to love her. I'm going down. There's not much doubt there. I just want to keep Blaire as clear from the wreckage as possible.

Chris is folding up the couch when I step into the living room. He gives me a nod and a grimace, and I know he's heard my half of the conversation.

I called him after Detective Diaz was here and told him everything. He's been here every night since. It's a nice gesture on his part, circling the wagons, but I really just needed to make sure he knows what needs to happen with rent and finances before this whole thing blows sky high and I'm not here to deal with it.

"Caiden—" Her voice chokes off on a sob. "No."

"Listen, Blaire. Detective Diaz is right. There's nothing either of us can do now to change whatever is going to happen, so stop trying to protect me." I screw my eyes shut in a grimace as my next words burn on their way up my throat. "I made a mistake. This whole thing was a huge mistake."

There's a long silence where all I hear is Blaire's shaky breath. "What are you saying?"

"I'm saying I never should have touched you." I swallow the pulsing lump in the back of my throat so she won't hear it in my words. "I'm saying I wish I never did."

"You don't mean that." Her voice is low, and mixed into the pain I hear an undercurrent of anger.

Good.

I glance at Chris, but then away when it's clear from his expression that hearing what I'm saying is almost as painful as saying it. "Christ, Blaire. Believe me, I do. I was stupid enough to let a firm ass and spectacular tits cloud my judgment."

"Jesus, Cade," Chris hisses and the same time Blaire says, "I thought—"

I cut them both off. "And it sure as hell didn't help that you lied to me," I tell her, hardening my wavering resolve.

My phone vibrates and I look at the screen. Mom.

When it rains, it fucking pours.

"I've got another call," I tell Blaire before she can offer up any argument. "Don't call me again."

I click over and can't dig a word out of the black tar of my soul to answer. I drop onto the couch and wait.

"Caiden?" Mom shrieks across the airwaves. "Are you there?"

"Is everything okay?" I finally manage.

"You tell me! The police were here earlier. They were asking questions about a seventeen-year-old girl they say you sodomized. They had *video*!"

Video. I feel the molten tar solidify and crack as all my insides freeze solid.

"What did you do!" she screeches.

And here we go. This is all the proof she needs that I'm my father. "I made a mistake."

The truth is, maybe I'm more like him than I ever wanted to admit. He fucked a seventeen-year-old when he was forty. I'm twenty-five. A few years difference, but it's all the same in the eyes of the law.

"A *mistake*?" she shrieks. "That's what you call it? You sodomized a baby, Caiden! I suppose you're going to do what your father did and tell me it was her fault? That she seduced you? You were a helpless victim?"

I close my eyes and loll my head onto the back of the sofa. "No, Mom. I'm no victim."

"Well, I told the detective who showed me the video that it looked pretty clear cut to me. I told her she should arrest you."

My heart lodges in my throat. I know it's coming, but that's still my body's reaction anytime I think about it. "I think they were planning on it without your endorsement, but thanks for the support, Mom. I really appreciate it."

There's a pound on my door. Mom is still shrieking through the airwaves as Chris goes to answer it. I put the phone down and tug on a T-shirt, then pick it up when, on the other side of the door is Detective Diaz along with one of East Overton's finest. The uniformed cop has his hand on the butt of his sidearm.

"Mom, I've got to go," I say.

Detective Diaz steps past Chris, a pair of handcuffs in her hand. "You'll need to end your call, Mr. Brenner."

"Is that them?" Mom asks. "Are they arresting you?"

Chris takes the phone from my hand. "Mom?" he asks.

He's listening the entire time it takes Detective Diaz to cuff me. Finally, as I'm being led out the door, he says, "You need to get over yourself Mom," and hangs up. "What do you need me to do?" he calls to me over Detective Diaz, who's reading my rights as I'm being led down the stairs.

I twist to look at him over my shoulder. "You've got my ATM and the credit card. Just take care of yourself."

"Shit," he says under his breath, then louder. "Fucking shit!"

I hear him banging down the stairs behind us. "Go inside, Chris." When he just stands there at the bottom of the stairs, his expression a mask of shock as the uniformed cop presses on my head and lowers me into the backseat of the waiting cruiser, I resort to the lie I promised myself I wouldn't tell. "It's going to be fine."

He stands there shaking his head as Detective Diaz asks if I understand my rights. I nod even though I didn't hear a word.

Very few of my neighbors come out to watch the spectacle. Even the bangers who are always in the parking lot are gone. Most of them probably have outstanding warrants, so they aren't going to push their luck. But I see tattered blinds being bent further out of shape as they watch from their crack house windows.

This is it, I think to myself as the cop slams the door on any future I might have had. *This is where my whole life derails.*

I slump low in my seat and loll my head against the window. But just as I'm closing my eyes, I see a silver Mini Cooper race past and skid to a stop in front of my apartment. As the cruiser takes a corner, I catch the briefest glimpse of long sable hair emerging from the driver's door right where Chris is still standing.

I drop my head against the headrest and swallow the hot lump in the back of my throat. Because I still don't regret a minute with her.

CHAPTER 17

Blaire

I nearly knock a guy standing at the bottom of Caiden's stairs over as I bolt for his apartment, but I'm only halfway up the stairs when I see the door is hanging wide open.

"Caiden!" I call, panic making my voice thick.

"He's gone," the guy says, turning toward me. He looks shell-shocked, his eyes glassy and his jaw hanging slack. He's tall and lanky. Somewhere between Caiden and Marcus, and his dirty blond hair is cut short.

I turn and descend a stair, trying to convince myself Caiden took my advice and ran. "What do you mean, gone?"

He shakes his head and blinks a few times, seeming to regain his footing. "Are you Blaire?"

I nod, my bloodstream suddenly full of ice water. "Where is he?"

He starts up the stairs. "Come on in."

I move to the side as he passes and as I get a closer look at his face, I recognize the mouth, lips the color of coral and fuller on the left. "Chris."

It's not a question, but he slows and nods.

I follow him up the stairs and close the door as he goes to the kitchen. "I've got coffee, Coke…" He opens the fridge and peers inside. "OJ?"

"Coffee is good," I say. I realize how hard I'm shaking when I hear it in my voice.

He pours a couple of cups and pushes one across the island to me.

I move across the room and take it.

"You're the one who got him into this," he says over the top of his mug.

I nod, still not trusting my voice. He's right to hate me. I hate myself.

But as he walks past me and drops onto the sofa, he looks aggravated but not particularly mad.

"I'm sorry," I manage after a long swallow of coffee.

His eyes snap to mine. "Caiden's not."

I don't know what to say to that. I move to the sofa and sit on the end away from him, focusing all of my attention on the dark liquid swirling in the mug, as if the key to everything lays in the non-existent leaves at the bottom, and I could see it if I looked hard enough.

"Listen," he says into the awkward silence. "Caiden didn't tell me a whole lot about what happened between you two, but he's a pretty level headed guy. If he took the risk, he must have decided you were worth it."

I look up at him and find eyes more blue and less storming than Caiden's looking back at me. But the shape is the same, as is the depth in them.

I clear my throat. "He said this was going to happen. He asked me to stay away from him."

"But then he came to you because *he* couldn't stay away. He told me that much." He tips his head back and empties his mug. "All I know for sure is the way he looked when he talked about you...like you were his reason for waking up every day." His eyes find mine again. "I'm not going to put words in his mouth if he didn't say them himself, but I've never seen him talk that way about anyone else. Ever."

A tear slips over my lashes despite the dam I've constructed. "I should have left him alone."

"I don't think he'd be any happier." He stands and takes my mug, going back to the kitchen and filling them both. "Are you going to want more?" he asks, lifting my mug. "'Cause this is the end of it."

"No thanks."

He moves around the end of the island and hands mine to me. "For what it's worth, I hope you don't give up on him," he says, sinking into his side of the sofa.

I think about the poem I'm in the middle of. *Girl Unhinged*. I remember the feeling that inspired it: euphoria so absolute that it couldn't be contained. This misery is just as absolute.

But I won't give up on Caiden. I can't.

CHAPTER 18

Caiden

"I've looked over your case file, Mr. Brenner," the court appointed lawyer sitting across the interrogation room table says to me. He's about my age in a threadbare gray suit. Totally unpretentious. I immediately trust the guy. "Your situation is serious. They've got an eyewitness on both counts, and the problem is, it's the lewd acts count that's backed with video evidence. Our only reasonable defense here is if we can prove you had plausible reason to believe Miss"— he glances down at the file—"Leon was eighteen."

I lean on my elbows. "There's no point pleading anything but guilty. We did everything they say we did and more, and I knew how old she was when we did it. I don't want Blaire dragged through a trial."

He nods slowly. "Then, I think we're right to plead it out, but we definitely don't want to go with a guilty plea on the lewd acts count. That would mandate that you file as a sex offender for life. It would preclude you from any number of jobs. Misdemeanor statutory rape doesn't carry that mandate." He leans back in his chair, splaying his hand on my file. "Miss Leon is adamant that the sex was consensual. In the state of California, consent doesn't matter in cases involving minors, but combined with the fact that she was seventeen it will probably sway the judge to try the case as a misdemeanor versus a felony. I suggest we plea to misdemeanor statutory rape and ask the lewd acts count be dropped."

"I'll go with whatever you say, as long as it keeps Blaire from having to be involved at all."

"You need to understand, there might be jail time…a few months maybe, but based on the strength of their evidence, I think that's the best we're going to do."

I nod.

"So, we're good?"

I'm in love with you, Caiden.

I close my eyes and breathe away the memory. "Yeah."

I'm so fucking far from good there's not a word. It's like some kind of cosmic joke, that the only woman I've ever truly loved isn't technically a woman at all in the eyes of the law. They say you can't choose who you love, but if I could, I'd choose Blaire every single time.

And every single time, it would ruin both our lives.

It's been three days since they hauled me out of my apartment in cuffs. I haven't shaved and I'm sure I look like shit. Not that I really care. There are only the lawyers, the judge, the court reporter, and me in the room for the arraignment. I sit, numb, as the prosecutor lays out their case for the judge, who watches the video and decides there's enough to hold me for trial.

"The defendant will be released on ten thousand dollars bail pending trial. We'll try it in closed court and seal the records due to the age of the victim." He looks at my lawyer. "How much time do you need for discovery?"

He glances at me and I nod. "Your honor, my client is prepared to enter a guilty plea to misdemeanor statutory rape provided the prosecution agrees to drop the lewd act with a minor charge."

The judge looks down at his case file. "The victim is sixteen?" he asks.

"Seventeen at the time of the alleged statutory rape, Your Honor," my lawyer answers.

He thumbs through a few pages, then looks at the prosecutor. "I'm inclined to say, based on what I've seen here, that would be my preliminary opinion. Do you have any evidence beyond what I've seen that would persuade me toward a different decision?"

"No, Your Honor. The prosecution would agree to the defense's plea."

The judge gives a nod, then looks at my lawyer. "Would you like a separate sentencing hearing, or can we do it here?"

My lawyer leans toward me. "We're not likely to get a more lenient judge by waiting, and it will just drag things out."

"Whatever you think."

"If your honor is ready to rule, we're agreeable to sentencing now," he says to the judge.

"Very well," the judge says. "If you'd stand, Mr. Brenner."

I do.

"Caiden Patrick Brenner, I hereby sentence you to two months jail time, followed by six months informal probation, and continuation of the court ordered restraining order. You are not to come within fifty yards of the minor…" He looks down at his records. "…Blaire Alison Leon, or attempt to contact her through any means, until she turns eighteen. At that point, it will be her choice whether to continue the order."

CHAPTER 19

Blaire

They didn't use my name in the newspaper article about Caiden's arrest. They do that to protect the identity of the minor involved. Maybe that's the way it's supposed to work, but in reality, word gets out anyway. I watched it start as a ripple my first day back at school—just whispered rumors in the hallways. By the end of the school day it had become a tsunami—the only thing people were talking about. Once it starts, there's no way of stopping it.

The last two weeks have been the juiciest the Oak Crest High gossip mill has ever seen. There have been days I wanted to stay in bed, but each morning I've peeled myself out of my dreams to go live the nightmare. I wish they'd call me a whore, or a slut. That, I could handle. I've got comebacks for all the slut slamming that goes on here.

But I hate that they're making me out as the victim—like I'm too stupid and naïve to understand that I was being taken advantage of. Raped.

I get sympathetic looks from teachers I've never had. Girls who I've never been friends with come up and give me hugs. When anyone's brave enough to say anything to my face, like a couple of the basketball guys I sort of know from class, it's always about how they hope Caiden gets raped in jail or something.

They think they're being supportive. All their really doing is killing me a little more inside with each comment.

I didn't want to go to graduation, but Mom pointed out that that would be a victory for the rumor mongers. "You're giving the valedictory speech, honey," she said when I told her. "This is your chance to show them that they haven't broken you."

So I take my place in front of the mic, lower my head and breathe, like I always do before slams. It's not dark. On the contrary, we're on the football field in the broad daylight of a sweltering June evening, so it's hot, sticky, and unbearably bright.

There's a TV news crew set up in the parking lot with one of those mobile dishes. They aren't supposed to know who I am, but that's not going to stop them from doing one of those inspirational human interest spots they slip into the news so it doesn't all seem so fucking depressing. "Despite horrendous adversity (that for legal reasons we are unable to disclose) local teen survives and perseveres," or whatever.

It just makes me more determined to say what I have to say.

I lift my head and focus on a random point, the same way I do at Tino's. "We all come into this world with a script that the great playwright, Society, has written for us. First scene, Act One is birth. Those lines don't require too much rehearsal, so most of us don't mess them up too badly." I ignore the smattering of laughter and press forward. "From there we've got a few soliloquies, but most of the script is dialogue. With family, friends, authority figures, adversaries. Some of it might seem mundane, but there's a lot to get through before the grow old and die scenes at the end of Act Five: Love, heartbreak, more love, disappointment, sex, more heartbreak, triumph, more love, more sex, marriage, kids, joy, more disappointment.

"And don't miss the underlying subtext in some of Society's scenes. There's his 'first love' scene, which, if you look closely, comes before the 'first sex' scene. And read carefully because, though Society hasn't cast those scenes for us and it's not mandated that each is performed with the same player, there are carefully outlined parameters for whom each scene can happen with. The consequences for choosing 'wrong' might throw the rest of the players into chaos. Then Society is left with no choice but to punish the one who derailed his carefully written script.

"But don't let me frighten you. Following the script is easy, especially when everyone around you is reading off the same one. When we all stick to Society's script, he's happy. He needs focused and disciplined players for everyone to get all the way to Act Five with no major hiccups. As long as no one deviates from their lines, then nothing could possibly go wrong, right?

"But here's a question that begs an answer: Who the hell is this 'Society' asshole who wrote the script? Who is he to choose who I can be friends with or who I'm allowed to love? I want to meet that sanctimonious prick because, I'm telling you, it must be one pretty fine high horse he's riding.

"What if I decide his script sucks and I let my heart write one that really speaks to me? What if I love outside the lines? Will Society turn his back on me? Would that be a bad thing? Or would it be empowering to live by my own standards instead of bowing to his?"

I push away from the podium. "So, to the graduating class of 2015, I say burn the fucking script. Write your own and to hell with Society and his high horse."

I turn and walk off the stage back to my seat and stunned silence.

I fight to keep my eyes on the superintendent—who's wearing makeup for the camera crew and is now at the podium doing damage control—to stop myself from looking for Caiden. I know he's not here. He's in prison. Because of me and Society's fucked up script.

He didn't tell me he loved me, but I swear I felt it in his kiss, his touch. I wish I could ask him if any of it was real, but with the restraining order, I won't be asking him anything for at least another year.

Neither Mom nor Dad say anything about my speech on the way home. I skip the party and go to straight to my room. I throw my regalia on the floor and tug on a soft T-shirt, then climb into bed. I lay in the dark with my earbuds in, listening to the Arctic Monkeys on repeat until my mind winds down. I sink into a restless sleep with images of Caiden flashing through my mind: a secret smile from the resource desk, his eyes on me as I read onstage, chocolate ice cream, the hot aching need in my belly as he lays on top of me.

I feel him there, his body hard and coiled against mine. His breath hot on my neck.

His fingers slip inside me. My hips rock to his rhythm.

"You want it bad, baby girl, don't you?"

The words seep into the periphery of the image, become part of the dream. "Yes," I whisper as I spread wider for him.

"I've missed you so fucking much," he says, sinking his dick into me.

I open my eyes as a sudden jolt of cold fear wrenches the sleep from my body.

Nate hooks his elbows through my knees, bending me into a pretzel and forcing my legs so far open that my hips are on the edge of dislocating. He grunts as he drives himself deep inside me, and the breath in my face is sour with something that smells like it probably went down sweet. Something stronger than beer.

"No, Nate!" I cry, trying to push him off. We may be the same height, but he's outweighs me by at least forty pounds of solid muscle.

He keeps his elbows through my knees and straightens his arms, wedging his hands under my ass. He's got my thighs plastered to the mattress on either side of me and my knees in my armpits, curling me onto a ball and forcing my ass into the air. His chest presses hard on mine as he supports his weight there and leverages to drive himself deeper inside me. His hips come down hard against my pelvis and there's a pop followed by searing pain in my right hip as it's twisted out of shape. I cry out.

"That's it, baby girl. You're feeling me?" He pulls out, his full body weight pressing down on my chest and crushing me. I can't breathe. Then he pounds hard into me, over and over.

"You—are—mine," he growls with each thrust, as if marking his territory.

Fear takes physical form as a barbed thing in my throat, choking off my protests. I struggle against him and gasp ineffectually for air. There's no breath to scream, or even cry out.

Spots flash in my eyes and the room starts to spit as I slowly suffocate under his weight. When I can't find anymore strength to fight, my arms fall limp to the bed at my sides. The pain in my body starts to fade with the sounds of his grunts.

Tears sting my eyes and run down my temples in rivulets, pooling in my ears. "Please stop," I whisper on my last breath.

Finally, he does. He thrusts twice more before collapsing on top of me. "Fuck yeah, baby girl," he groans in my ear. "Just fuck yeah."

I'm still pinned beneath him. My legs are numb. My hands tingle. The only air I can get is in tiny pants. The only part of my mangled body I can move is my neck. I turn my head and close my eyes as tears pour through my hair and soak my pillowcase.

After an endless minute, Nate climbs off me. Sharp needles begin to prick my legs with the return of blood flow. White hot pain cuts through my hips and back as I roll on my side, away from him, but I swallow the gasp. I listen to him pull on his clothes and pray sincerely to God for the mattress to open up and swallow me.

I flinch a minute later when he leans down and kisses my cheek. "Love you, baby girl." Then the door clicks closed.

I sob into my pillow until yellow light breaks through my curtains hours later.

Nate and Marcus are downstairs. I don't even know what time it is, but I've been laying here listening to them for what feels like hours. Every time I hear Nate's voice, all my insides pull tight and my lungs feel like they're being crushed again.

I'm never leaving this room.

Excited shouts erupt from downstairs. A second later, Marcus is banging on my door, calling my name. I pull the sheets over my head when the door is thrown open.

"You're on the fucking news!" he shouts. "They're bleeping the shit out of you! You gotta see this."

I roll toward the window and bunch the pillow under my head. "I was there, so I think I'm good."

He yanks me to my feet. "My sister's fucking famous."

A dagger shoots through my right hip with the motion and I cry out with the pain.

"You okay?" he asks, his eyes scanning me with sudden concern.

No. I look at him a long moment, wanting so badly to say it, but I can't make my mouth form the word. Marcus wasn't as understanding as my mother when everything with Caiden came to light. He wanted to kill Caiden. I got pissed at him for doing the same thing everyone else has been doing—judging Caiden based on things that have nothing to do with how we are together. Marcus was the person who understood me better than anyone else—the one person I was sure would be there to lean on. And he wasn't. Things have been strained between us for the last couple of weeks. How much worse would it get if he knew I've been fucking Nate?

"It was just a rough night," is what comes out when I finally open my mouth.

He bites his lips in a self-conscious gesture. "What you fucking did up there...it was brilliant, Blaire." He squints a question at me. "You really loved that Caiden guy?"

A tear slips over my lashes. "I still do."

He scratches the top of his head. "It's just really hard for me to think about some fucking guy doing…*that* to you." Finally, his eyes lift to mine. "We're all dicks, Blaire. We don't even need to *like* you to fuck you. I just don't want some guy taking advantage of you." He shakes his head. "Doesn't matter how old he is. Doesn't matter who he is. I'd want to fucking kill the guy."

He spreads his arms and I step into them.

"What the hell are you wearing?" he asks after a second.

"I was cold," I say, my hands bunching into the layers of cotton and fleece at my hips. I got up during the night and pulled on four layers of sweatpants and three sweatshirts.

He grins and throws me over his shoulder. I gasp with the pain in my hip but bite back the scream. "You've got to come see yourself. We TiVoed it."

Marcus carries me down the stairs and sets me on my feet. Nate is on the floor with a throw pillow bunched behind his head. I nearly turn around when sends me his dimpled grin. Marcus sprawls himself over the sofa and yanks me down to sit on his stomach, then picks up the remote.

"Back it up, dude," Nate says.

"What the fuck do you think I'm doing?" Marcus shoots back as the footage of me at the graduation mic speeds by in reverse.

He hits play and I get to watch myself tell the world off. It only makes me feel sicker when Nate winks at me.

"Where are Mom and Dad?" I ask when Marcus and Nate finally stop with the commentary several minutes later.

Marcus shrugs. "Fuck if I know. They were gone when we got up." He slides me off him and peels himself out of the sofa. "I'm gonna hit the shower." He crumples an empty Coke can and chucks it at Nate. "You heading home, dude?"

Nate pelts the can back at Marcus and drags himself off the floor. "Yeah. We partying tonight?"

"Always," Marcus says, striding for the stairs. "Catch you later."

I go to the kitchen without looking at Nate, because I've suddenly broken out in a cold sweat despite my layers of clothing. I hope he'll take the hint and leave, but he follows me into the kitchen.

My whole body seizes when he leans in behind me, where I'm hiding in the refrigerator. "I was thinking…maybe we should come clean with Marcus."

A cold stone fist squeezes my stomach and I swallow back bile. I feel my hands start to shake. I wrap them around my middle and clench them into my sweats. "Come clean?"

If he tells my brother he raped me, I don't even want to think about what Marcus would do.

He pulls himself up to sit on the counter. "I think we should date, baby girl. Make it official."

"How much did you drink last night?" I ask, pulling a blueberry yogurt off the shelf and closing the fridge.

He grins. "You missed a crazy fucking graduation party, that's for sure, but I'm serious. I like you. We're good together. And if fucking Marcus can't get over himself and be good with that, then fuck him."

I look more closely at him as I move behind the table with my yogurt, putting an obstacle between us. There's no hint of humor in his eyes.

I stir my yogurt but when I bring the spoon to my mouth the thought of putting anything in there makes me gag. "I'm serious, Nate," I say, staring at the spoon. "I need to know how drunk you were when you came into my room last night."

His dimples pop as a slow smile curves his lips. "Not so drunk that I don't remember how you rocked my fucking world."

A tear slips over my lashes and courses a crooked path down my cheek. "I didn't want to have sex with you last night, Nate. I said no."

The smile falls off his face and his eyes widen. "You said yes. I *definitely* remember that."

"I was mostly asleep when I said that." I lower the spoon and scrub the back of my hand over my face. "But when I woke up, I said no. I asked you to stop. I tried to push you away."

I stiffen as he slips off the counter and lowers himself into the chair across from me. "Baby girl, I'd never hurt you. I…didn't hear. I swear."

I flinch when he reaches for my arm.

"Fuck," he growls under his breath. I lift my head when I see him stand and pace toward the family room. "You don't know what it was like, hearing what that cocksucker did to you. I want to rip his fucking dick off for fucking with you."

A cold shiver fingers up my spine with the realization that this is what last night was about. Nate didn't like that I fucked someone else.

"He didn't fuck with me. I *wanted* to sleep with him." I spin on Nate, suddenly finding a small reservoir of strength hidden inside the memory of how Caiden made me feel. "*He* didn't rape me. *You* did."

He lowers his eyes and rubs them. "I don't even know what else to say, except I'm serious, Blaire." He lifts his gaze to mine again, and I'm not sure what I see there. Remorse? Or just fear. "I really like you. I've never felt like this about anyone else. Just give me a chance to make it up to you, okay? We can slow way down. No sex. We can just hang out…spend some time together. Do normal shit, movies and whatever."

I feel my body go weak and start to shake as the little bit of strength I found evaporates. I go to the family room and sink into the sofa before my legs give out, curling into a ball in the corner and pulling my knees up, resting my forehead on them.

I can't begin to decipher what I'm feeling. He raped me, but it's Nate. *My* Nate. He was drunk. Maybe he really didn't hear me.

"I promise, Blaire," he says, from the doorway to the kitchen. "I won't touch you again until you ask me to. Okay?"

I feel myself nodding against my knees, though it's not a conscious gesture.

"Listen…I'm gonna go. Give you some space."

I stiffen as I see him in my peripheral vision, moving slowly closer, as if approaching a skittish animal. I work hard not to flinch again as he leans down and kisses the back of my head. "I'm sorry," he whispers in my ear.

Then he's gone.

CHAPTER 20

Caiden

Jail really isn't much like they make it out to be in the movies. There are no three hundred pound guys with bandanas and tattoos who want to make me their prison bitch, the guards seem like pretty regular guys, and I don't see much of a "black market" other than an old man who trades desserts for cigarettes that he keeps down his pants. Maybe it's because I'm in county instead of the state penitentiary, but it isn't all that bad. Rent's free, so there's that. The gym, where I spend most of my day, is decent and there's no monthly fee. The food's horrible, but so was most of what I cooked for myself, so I can't complain on that front.

Most everyone keeps their heads down, minds their own business, and does their time. But there are two guys on my block who have an issue with me, apparently. The bigger one is about my height and has a few pounds on me, but he's not as cut as Jones. He's got a beer gut and looks soft, so I'm pretty sure I could take him if push came to shove. The little one is maybe five seven and wiry. I could snap him like a toothpick. I call the little one Hans and the big one Franz because they watch me in the gym, though I've never once seen either of them lift a weight. Every time I walk within earshot, they grab their dicks and mutter things about fucking babies up the ass. I figure if I can steer clear for two more weeks, they're someone else's problem.

The buzzer sounds, waking us for another day. I wait for everyone to stream down the block to the cafeteria before I drag myself out of bed and grab my shower stuff. When I step into the bathroom, for once, there's no line. Three of the five shower stalls are taken, so I slip into the empty one on the far end. The guy next to me has a speaker in the shower with him, playing some loud, angry music that seems to vibrate at the resonance of my rage. I strip off my jumpsuit and hang it on the hook on the wall outside the curtain, then step into the water. I crank it hotter and just stand here with my hands braced against the tile wall, feeling the vibration of the music sink into my bones and letting all the shit slide off me and swirl down the drain.

In two weeks I go back out into a world where I have no place. All I've got that are in any way useful are my car and a Masters degree in comparative literature that I earned two years ago on my way to my doctorate. I'm sure Dr. Duncan would strip me of it he could, but the best he can do now is keep me from finishing my Ph.D. My dissertation is complete, but I missed my meeting with the board to defend it because I was in jail. If I want to reschedule it I have to appeal to the board, and since Dr. Duncan is the chairman, I'm fairly certain my appeal will be denied.

I know Chris would do anything I asked to help, but the problem is, I don't know what to ask for. He has been here like clockwork every visiting day. He officially moved in with Taryn last month and I guess they both plan to apply to Sierra State next year. He's building a life and I'm not going to screw with it.

I'm just reaching for my soap when something crashes through the plastic curtain, tearing it from the rod, and I'm slammed face first up against the wall. My forehead cracks sharply off the tile and I lose my bearings for a second as stars flash in my eyes.

"Hey, loverboy," a deep voice growls in my ear. Franz. "Since you like to fuck babies, we figured you were fair game."

My heart slams against the wall so hard I feel my body jerk to the rapid rhythm. *Fuck.* This can't be happening.

I struggle against Franz's grip, but the slick, wet skin of his beer gut is all up my back. He has me pinned to the wall with my right arm twisted behind me, his forearm across the back of my neck, and a knee between my legs.

"You got him?" comes the second voice. Hans. He sounds like he's on the floor.

"Yeah," Franz answers. "I got him. You go first."

A hand clamps around one of my ankles and my leg is ripped out from under me. It stops when my foot slams up against the side wall of the shower. I slip down the wall six inches and would go to the floor like a break dancer doing the splits if Franz wasn't holding me up. But my legs are now spread eagle and there's nothing I can do to close them.

"Move over," Hans says, just behind me now.

Franz shifts off to the side a little, and then a finger slides down my ass crack. "I've been watching this tight ass for a while," Hans says, his finger perched right at my asshole. He shoves it inside and my breath catches. "Fucking sweet. This is prime virgin ass. Everything I hoped it would be."

I struggle against Franz's grip as Hans withdraws his finger. His hands spread my ass cheeks and then the head of his goddamn hard-on is pressed up against my asshole. "Ready for me, sweet cheeks?"

On an electric surge of adrenaline, I rotate and bring my left elbow back hard in the direction of Hans's voice. There's a satisfying crunch when I feel it connect with bone. He wails from behind me and Franz lets up his grip just enough that, with a hard jerk, I'm out from under him.

Hans is on the floor holding his bleeding nose, but Franz gets his hands on me, trying to wrestle me into a headlock. I swing with an undercut that connects with his jaw. His head jerks back and he staggers. I finish him with a knee to the balls. I kick Hans in the face when he makes a grab for me, then bolt, leaving everything behind.

Two guys shaving at the bathroom mirrors watch me go.

"Thank you very fucking little for the help, assholes," I call over my shoulder.

When I pass through the gates back into my block at a stiff clip, the guard there looks at me funny then follows me to my cell.

"What's this about, inmate?" he says, waving a hand at my naked form.

I'm breathing hard as I drop onto my cot. "Thought I might wait until someone's not trying to rape me to finish showering."

His hand goes to the butt of his baton as he lifts his radio. "Detail to Block C showers."

"Roger that," a disembodied voice comes back.

"Stay here. I'll find you a towel." He turns and when he leaves, I hold my head in my hands while the adrenaline charging my blood begins to ebb.

So maybe I was wrong about this not being like in the movies.

"Here," the guard says a minute later, and a towel lands on the mattress next to my leg.

I shake it open and stand, wrapping it around my waist. "Those fuckers are a piece of work."

"You just described ninety percent of our population. Exactly which fuckers would those be?"

I shrug. "Don't know their names, just call them Hans and Franz."

He cracks a smile but quickly loses it. "If they're still in there, the detail will take care of them."

"Broke Hans's nose, pretty sure," I say, shaking my hand as pain just starts to register.

He juts his chin and nods. "How much longer you got?"

"Twelve days."

"I'm Don. I'll tell the guys to keep an eye on you. And if you point out Hans and Franz, we'll watch them too. Shit like this doesn't happen here."

I nod. "Appreciate it. Thanks."

"I'll go find your jumpsuit," he says, turning for the hall.

Twelve days later, they spit me out into a hot late-July day. Hannah is outside the gates, waiting to pick me up. She's the only one other than Chris who came to see me in prison. There was no one else I could call.

She pulls me into a hug. "You're free!" she says in my ear.

"Guess so."

We climb into her car. "Let me take you out for some real food," she says as she pulls away from the prison. "Luigi's? My treat, to celebrate."

I glance at her as my mouth starts to water. "That sounds really good. Thanks."

We find an open booth in the back. Once our orders are in, Hannah looks at me. "How bad was it?"

"Prison?" I shrug. "Other than the two guys who wanted a piece of my virgin ass, not too bad."

Her eyes widen. "Are you serious? Did they try anything?"

"They jumped me in the shower last week. My kickboxing came in handy."

"So they didn't...?"

"Naw. The guards were pretty cool. They kept an eye on me after that." I smile at her. "And then you came to my rescue."

The waiter drops our drinks and a basket of breadsticks on the table, then moves past.

Hannah grabs a breadstick and dips it in marinara. "Was she worth it?"

I take a deep breath and watch my fingers slowly spin my beer glass on the table. "Yes."

There's a long silence. "Do you miss her?"

I laugh under my breath even though there's nothing remotely funny. "Only when I'm breathing." My smile dies and I take a long swallow of beer. "She's about the freest spirit I've ever met, but not in a frivolous way. She's deep, and courageous, and incredibly insightful, and self-aware, and her mind works in ways I can't even fathom. She's fascinating."

"You *love* her."

I lift my eyes and nod.

"She sounds awfully mature for a sixteen-year-old."

"Seventeen…now."

"Seventeen," she repeats. "What's her home situation?"

I shrug. "Don't really know too much about it. Just that her parents are around, I guess, but still pretty absentee. She and her brother took care of each other growing up."

"Maybe that's why she's so mature," Hannah says, setting her beer down. "She had to learn responsibility early."

"Maybe."

"So, what are you going to do about her?"

I shake my head. "What are my choices? She won't be eighteen for another year. And…" I bite my lips between my teeth. "I'm not convinced the courts aren't right. Especially if your theory is true. If her parents have already stolen years off her childhood, who am I to take what's left?"

Her look goes all incredulous. "But you just admitted to loving her."

"That doesn't mean I have the right to be selfish." I tear off a hunk of breadstick with my teeth. "And at this point it really doesn't matter. I come within fifty yards of her in the next ten months, I go back to jail for at least three years. Maybe more."

Our dinners come and the waiter drops them onto our paper placemats.

"So tell her how you feel and ask her to wait," she says.

I cram a bite of lasagna in my mouth. "For a year?"

"Ten months."

"Ten more months of her childhood she'll never get back." I take another bite, chew, swallow. "When I was seventeen, I was getting drunk at post-football parties, going on awkward dates, shoplifting condoms with my guys, and jacking off to my buddy Joey's dad's Playboy magazines. I can't ask her to sit around and wait for me if it means missing her opportunity to experience those things."

"You're afraid she'll miss awkward dates and Playboy magazines?" she asks, raising her eyebrows.

"Yes. I don't want to deprive her of awkward dates."

I scarf down another huge wedge of lasagna and wash it down with the rest of my beer. I catch the waiter's eye and lift my empty glass. He heads to the bar for another.

She twirls some pasta onto her fork. "I would have given anything to skip seventeen."

"You can say that now because you've already lived through it. If you'd skipped it, you'd always wonder what you missed."

She looks at me another long minute as she chews. "Maybe," she concedes after she swallows.

When we're finished, she waves the waiter down and asks for the check. She scrapes her chair back and turns for the door. "Let's find a bar and get really fucking shitfaced. You have lost time to make up for."

We find a club on the next corner that's loud and packed, and wind our way through the crush of sweaty bodies to the bar. I'm on my fourth...or maybe fifth scotch when a blonde and a redhead come up and ask me to dance.

Hannah gives me a little shove toward them. "Go. This is your coming out party."

The blonde gives Hannah a look.

Hannah waves her hands. "He's not gay. He just got out of jail."

The blonde still looks wary, but a smile creeps over the redhead's face. I let her drag me to the dance floor. I realize I'm drunker than I thought when I more stagger than walk. After the first song, I'm done and excuse myself. When I find Hannah again, she grins at me. "Get any phone numbers?"

I shake my head. "Wasn't really feeling it."

She gives me a long, reprising look that I ignore. I down the rest of my scotch and when she sips her drink through a straw, I realize she's switched to club soda at some point.

"Come on, cowboy," she says, setting down her glass and grabbing the front of my shirt. She starts dragging me through the throng to the door. "Let's get you home."

She guides me to her car and sets me in the passenger seat. I sag against the door and sort of zone out...or maybe pass out, as she drives. The next thing I know, we're stopping.

"How was your first day of freedom?" she asks as she stands me up from the seat and loops an arm around my back.

I hook an elbow around her neck. "Being out doesn't suck as much as being in."

She half carries, half drags me into her apartment and lays me on the couch with a pillow and blanket. She sits on the edge and tucks the blanket around me. "What do you think you're going to do now?"

I glare up at her. "You're really going to make me sort my fucking life out this second? When I'm so fucked up I can't even see straight?"

It comes out slurred, but she seems to understand.

"Sometimes that's when you see the clearest," she says, holding my gaze.

There's only one thing I know I want, and I can't have it. "I have no fucking clue," I finally answer.

She bends and kisses me softly on the lips. "Sweet dreams, Philotes. I'll see you in the morning."

I wake in a puddle of sweat with eyes that are crusted shut. I have to rub the shit out of them before I can get them open. The sun is beating through the picture window of her family room and cooking me right to the couch. I pull myself up and find Hannah at the kitchen counter in a short bathrobe, mucking with the coffee pot.

"That ready?" I ask.

She turns and looks at me. "Morning, bright-eyes." She holds up a piece of curved black plastic. "And no. The doohickey that stops the coffee from dripping when you pull the carafe out came off and I can't get it back on."

I go over and inspect it for a minute, then snap the pieces back together in the only way it looks like they could go. "That look right?" I ask, handing it back. She slides it into the machine and it clicks in. "Looks like it."

She presses the start button and as it percolates, even just the smell makes me feel more human. "Thanks for last night. It was good to be in the world again."

She slips into a seat at her small kitchen table and checks her phone. She texts something and looks up at me, where I'm waiting near the coffee maker. "I think you should file an appeal with the dissertation board."

"What would be the point? All I wanted my PhD for was so I could teach. I'll have to disclose my statutory rape conviction on any job application I file. No university is going to hire me."

"You worked for too long just to give up."

There are at least two cups worth of coffee in the pot, so I yank it out and fill the two mugs Hannah left on the counter. "It was gone the second I decided to fuck Blaire behind the stacks." Though I don't remember ever making that conscious decision. I just remember getting so lost in her nothing else mattered.

I bring her mug over to her and down half of mine in one swallow. It burns my mouth and throat, but I don't give a shit. It's the first real coffee I've had in two months, and nothing has ever tasted better.

"If you're not going to pursue teaching, then what are you going to do?"

I drop into the chair across from her. "You really *are* going to make me sort all this out right now, aren't you?"

"I just think you need to consider what your options are. You've got a bachelor's degree in English, right? And a master's in comparative lit? There have to be options."

"That don't involve working with anyone under eighteen? Not many. Schools, libraries, they're all out."

"My mother is the executive editor for Brandish Publishing. They do mostly trade magazines. Have you thought about writing? Or even editing?"

I know she's right. I need to start thinking about this. But right now, the toilet of my life has just finished flushing. All the shit has just swirled down the drain and it's nothing but empty. Maybe when the tank starts to fill again I'll be able to see potential options.

We put in a movie and Hannah stops pushing me to solve all my shit. When it's over, I lay on the couch with my elbow hooked over my eyes and bake some more while she showers and changes.

It's late in the afternoon when she drops me at my depressing apartment. It's almost comforting to find the same group of gang bangers hanging around their cluster of low-riders.

"My car's still here, so that's something," I say, stepping out of Hanna's car.

"You're going to be okay?" she asks, her eyes full of concern as they shoot to the bangers and back.

"Professor!" one of them calls. He grins as he raises a hand and metal teeth flash in the sun.

"Yeah," I say, leaning down and looking at her through the open passenger window. "My homies missed me."

"Call me later, okay?"

I nod. "Thanks for everything."

I turn and climb the stairs into my apartment, then crawl into bed and stay there for the next two days.

CHAPTER 21

Blaire

The global sick feeling, like toxic swamp mud oozing through my veins, has finally started to fade.

It started with a movie, just like Nate promised. He bought us a bucket of popcorn and a large soda to share, and about halfway through the flick, I reached for his greasy hand and held it in mine, just to prove to myself I could. Something about facing down my fears and wanting desperately for something in my life to feel normal again.

A week later, we went to the lake. When he asked why I didn't wear a swimsuit, I told him I was on my period. I sat in the sun and sweated in my jeans and sweatshirt, afraid if I showed Nate too much of myself, he might get the idea I was good to go. But by the end of the day, when he ran up onto the beach soaking wet and shook himself all over me like a dog, I swallowed the current of electric terror and I let him kiss me.

Two weeks ago, he took me for a burger and we made out in his car after. I gripped the upholstery and let him touch me through my clothes. When he brought me home, he told Marcus we were dating.

Marcus still isn't speaking to either of us.

I have to say, the fact that Nate's risked his brotherhood with Marcus for me says more than anything else he could have done. I mean more to him than even Marcus. But it hurts that it's driven Marcus and I even farther apart. I feel like I'm floating alone in the world with no one but Nate.

Since then, we've gone to parties together and started hanging out with Zoey and some kids from my graduating class who decided I was cool after my graduation speech. We've made out and there's been some groping, but he hasn't pushed for sex.

Nate tells everyone he's my boyfriend. I'm starting to get used to it. I'm pretty sure now that if he'd heard me say no on graduation night, he would have stopped.

Nate brought me to Tino's tonight. I'm feeling way more emotional than usual, like I'm living just on the edge of tears, because this is my last slam. By the fourth Friday in August, I'll be in Berkeley.

I'm second to last tonight, so we sit at a table near the front with some of the other poets and I hug each of them after they read. When Craig starts to announce me, I already feel the hot press of tears behind my eyes. I'll be lucky to make it through without choking up onstage. I scrape my chair back, but as I turn toward the stage stairs, Nate stands and grabs my hand. He pulls me back to him with his full-throttle smile and tucks me against his hard body. "Kick some ass, baby girl," he says, then kisses me long and hard.

I give him a weak smile when he lets me go and move to the stage. Craig grabs my hand at the top of the stairs. "We're going to miss you," he says as he squeezes, then his smile fades. "*I'm* going to miss you."

I smile back and step up to the mic. I lower my head and breathe before looking up into the dark room and fixating on a spot over the bar.

I start; it's a poem about sacrifice and compromise tonight. I'm on a roll when a dark figure passes through my focal point on the back wall. My eyes catch on him and when he looks up as he reaches the door, it's Caiden's face staring back at me.

I stumble over my words and he stalls in the door, as if he's looking for some way to catch me before I fall. I take a deep breath and recover my spot, and as I finish my poem, he slips away.

My heart screams at me to chase him. To catch him. To hold him and never let him go. But my feet remain rooted to the stage. Because my head knows that he could be arrested for even being here.

We were notified when he got out of prison three days ago. I know what will happen if he comes near me. His misdemeanor would revert to a felony and he'd go back to jail for at least three years. When he finally got back out, he'd have to register as a sex offender for the rest of his life.

It's not until Craig hands me a tissue that I realize tears are streaming down my face. When I can finally move, he helps me down the stage stairs with an arm around my waist.

Nate takes me out of his arms at the bottom and guides me back to my seat. "You okay, babe?"

"Yeah, I just…" I sip my soda and will my mind to stop spinning. "This is my last slam before I leave for school. I'm going to miss it."

Nate pulls me to his shoulder. "There's no way you won't be able to find a slam in East Bay. There's got to be dozens of them."

"I know, but these guys are my family."

Gloria takes my hand and squeezes it. "Won't be the same without you here, girlfriend."

The last poet reads and the lights come up. There's a line of people waiting to hug me or say goodbye, but I can't help watching the door for Caiden. Nate is impatient and finally tugs me toward the door by my arm. I wave at the rest of the group as he pulls me outside.

"I was fucking roasting in there," he says, towing me down the street to where he parked.

I look around, but I don't see Caiden or his car. And I'm glad. It hacked a chunk out of my heart, seeing him standing in that room.

Nate drives me home, and when we get to my bedroom door, he takes my hand and pulls me through.

Caiden looked me right in the eye and walked away tonight. But Nate is here. Nate has always been here.

He kisses me as he backs me toward the bed. We strip without a word and he rolls a condom on. He turns off the light and I lay back on the bed. I close my eyes as he lays on top of me. He spreads my knees with his and something clamps hard in my stomach. I turn my head to the side so the pools in my eyes leak onto the pillow as he guides himself inside me.

"Just like coming home, babe," he moans.

He fucks me slowly and kisses my wet face.

"Shh, baby," he whispers when I whimper.

He comes with a groan a few minutes later and rolls off me.

I lay my head on his chest and listen to his heartbeat. I try to shut off my mind, but Caiden's face is there, his blue eyes storming into mine. He's got his own gravitational pull, and I'm his moon. I felt it the whole evening at Tino's—an itchy restless feeling I couldn't define—and when I saw him, I understood. My soul knew he was there the whole time. It was reaching for his. If I let myself slingshot alone through space, I will find my way back to him.

He made his choice. He walked away tonight. He doesn't think I'm worth the risk.

So I wrap my arms around Nate and cling tightly to the only other planet that has any draw over me at all to keep the universe in balance.

CHAPTER 22

Caiden

If I get caught here, Hans and Franz are going to be very happy. Because three years is a long time to have to fight them off when I get my ass thrown back in jail for violating the restraining order.

I slip into Tino's after the slam starts because I know it will be dark. I grab a stool in the back and order a double scotch, which I pound in a shot before ordering a second.

I recognize most of the people at the table up front with Blaire. Three of them are regular poets here. But the stalky brown-haired guy is new. He might have a few years on Blaire, but there's no way he's older than twenty. He's about her height, so maybe five nine, but he's built like a linebacker.

I watch them together: she, fidgeting with her hands in her lap, watching the stage and occasionally sipping her soda; he, always leaning toward her, always with a possessive hand on her leg, her back, in her hair. Whispering in her ear.

I want to know what he's saying to her.

That Craig guy begins her intro and she stands and starts toward the stage, but the boyfriend yanks her back by the arm. I'm off the stool before I realize it, hating the way he's manhandling her. But I rein myself back as he crushes her against him, laying his claim for everyone to see. They kiss, long and hard, and everything inside me seizes.

There is something seriously wrong with me. Maybe I really am the child molester everyone thinks I am, because I can't stop obsessing over her. It's been two months. Jail, probation, restraining orders—you'd think something would have been enough of a deterrent to cure me of my addiction. But no. I've been out of prison for three days, and here I am, already breaking my parole.

But Blaire is insidious, weaving herself into my DNA with unbreakable bonds. I put a tub of chocolate ice cream in my cart at the market yesterday and caught myself smiling. Some random girl in whatever mindless show I was watching last night twirled the ends of her hair around her finger and something warmed in my chest.

But she's moved on.

She's onstage, but suddenly being in this room with her is ripping out my soul. I toss back my third scotch and stand. I move to the door, but when I get there, I can't help myself from glancing back—one last image of the girl who blew my mind to burn into my memory.

And her gaze levels me.

She steals my breath and freezes me in place with those sad whiskey eyes.

She stumbles on her words and the impulse to rush up there and catch her fall is so overpowering that it cracks the ice in my veins and propels me a step in her direction.

Before I remember that I can't go to her.

Ever again.

She closes her eyes and takes a breath, then picks up the line she stumbled over and finishes from there.

She *recovers*.

Because that's what normal people do when everything goes sideways. They pick up all their shit and make something that doesn't stink.

I push out the door onto the sidewalk and stagger to my car. I climb in and find myself at Hannah's without remembering anything about the drive.

She opens the door a crack, then wider when she sees it's me. "Hey," she says with a curious raise of her eyebrows.

It's late and she's in a short bathrobe, as if she might have been on her way to the shower. I push through the door and lift her off her feet, devouring her mouth as if it's my last meal. She kicks the door closed and wraps her long legs around my waist. I carry her to the bedroom.

And do everything in my fucking power to recover.

CHAPTER 23

Blaire

School keeps me busy. Busy is good. Less time to think.

I bust my ass studying and only manage Bs in most of my first semester classes. Berkeley is a world away from high school…and even Sierra State, where the grading seemed a little more lenient.

Nate is in Reno, a six-hour drive from Berkeley, so we only manage to see each other when we are both home for Thanksgiving. His mother invites Marcus and me over for Thanksgiving dinner, but Marcus still isn't speaking to Nate, so we stay home with our parents and go out to Denny's instead. Mom's never seen the point of cooking a huge turkey for just the four of us.

Nate and I text every day, and I call him on the nights I'm feeling Caiden's gravitational pull trying to crush my heart to a pulp against my ribcage. Hearing Nate's voice grounds me in my reality. A reality I have to accept.

But as I drive home for winter break, the closer I get to home—to Caiden—the more I feel it. I stay on the highway an extra few exits and take the long way home through East Overton. It's after nine when I pull up to his complex. The streetlights near his complex are all out, and low roiling cloud cover charges the air and makes me edgy. My hands shake on the wheel as I drive slowly through the dark parking lot. My heart breaks into a gallop when I see his car in a spot near his apartment. Upstairs, his bedroom light is on and the shade is open. I back into a parking space across the lot, where I've got a clear view of the window, and turn off the engine.

He can't be arrested for *me* stalking *him*, right?

I convince myself I only need a glimpse of him. Then I can go home and live my sorry excuse for a life. I'll give it fifteen minutes. If he hasn't come to the window in that time, I'll leave. I recline my seat back and wait.

It's nearly two hours later when a bare-chested Caiden appears in the window. My heart lurches me forward, pressing my chest against the steering wheel in an attempt to get closer.

He's grown a beard—short and golden blond, a few shades lighter than the honey brown waves on his head. And he's been working out. His body was amazing before, but now he's ripped. I etch the image into my memory as he reaches up to pulls the blinds.

But he lowers his hand when a tall blonde wraps her arms around his shoulders from behind. She's nearly his height, and is wearing a thin white cami. She says something close to his ear and he turns in her arms.

A stone fist crushes my heart when she grasps a handful of his hair and yanks him to her, kissing him hard. He reaches for the blinds again when she lets him go, and the window goes dark.

All I can do is stare at where he was for another minute, his image still outlined on my retinas. I close my eyes as tears hitch up my throat.

I never expected Caiden would wait around for a year for me. I'm with Nate. Of course he's found someone else. He's beautiful and smart and incredible. What did I think he was going to do, become a monk?

I breathe back the tears and almost have it together when a loud bang on my window makes me jump. I look up to see a guy with gold teeth shining out of his depraved grin.

"Chica! Come out and play!" He pushes off my car and grabs his junk. "I got some toys you gonna like!"

Three more guys stalk my direction from farther down the parking lot. Gold Teeth jumps back when I start the car and peal out.

My shaking has started to subside by the time I pull up to the curb in front of the house twenty minutes later. But it's back when the car I pull up behind is Nate's. Over the course of the semester, Marcus and I have gradually gotten back to shooting texts at each other a couple times a day. But we never mention Nate. He's still the elephant in the room. As long as we ignore his existence, Marcus and I do okay. But as far as I know, Nate is still on Marcus's shit list.

I rush inside and find Nate and Marcus in the family room. They're wrestling on the floor, crashing into the coffee table and nearly knocking it over. There's a lot of grunting and cursing, but no one's laughing...so it looks like they're working things out in their own way.

I leave them to deal with each other and go to the shower.

Spring semester seems to drag. But that's mostly because I forgo any semblance of a social life and spend every waking minute holed up in the library or my room with my books. I'm down to my last final, but Nate just drove down from Reno today. He finished finals a few days earlier than me and came straight to Berkeley to stay with me while I finish up.

But I realize that might have been a really bad idea when I'm on the bed, trying to study, and he's sitting behind me, playing with my tits.

"Glad I didn't miss your birthday," he says in my ear. He takes my hand and lays it on his junk. "I've got a very special package with your name on it."

"Yeah, me too," I say, taking my hand off him. "But I really have to study this."

A key rattles in the lock just before my roommate, Aimee, pushes through the door into the room. She's all blond Malibu Barbie, which is a little scary because that's really where she's from.

"Well, look at that!" she says, smiling at Nate. "You exist!"

He gives her his full-dimple grin as he pats himself down. "Last I checked, yeah."

She drops her bag near her desk. "It's just, Blaire tells any guy that comes onto her she's got this boyfriend, but it's been an entire school year and no one's ever met you, so...you can see why we were a little skeptical."

He looks at me as if he doesn't like that someone might have been touching his stuff. "Guys hit on you?"

I shrug. "Sometimes."

Aimee drops onto her bed. "You've got nothing to worry about. Her nose is always in a book. If I can drag her to a party, it must be a freaking ice storm in hell."

Nate climbs off my bed. "Nate," he says, holding out a hand to Aimee. "The real live boyfriend. Great to meet you."

"You ready in there?" I hear Dee, who lives across the hall, call from the hallway. A second later, she comes through the open door with a...

"Is that a cake?" I ask, scooting off the bed.

She puts it on my desk and brushes her long afro off her face, leaving a smudge of white frosting across her black cheek. Her boyfriend, Mike, come through behind her and starts singing "Happy Birthday." He's tall, skinny, and blond. Dee's negative image.

Everyone joins in, even Nate, who hams it up, acting the song out like he's in some Broadway musical. I walk over and look at the sorriest excuse for a cake I've ever seen.

"Aimee couldn't get it out of the pan in one piece," Dee explains.

"You didn't grease the pan!" Aimee shoots back. "It stuck!"

Dee does a 'whatever' eye roll. "I had to glue it back together with frosting."

I stare at it, then crack up. Crumbs of chocolate cake are all mixed in with the white frosting, and the top layer has slid halfway off. Happy Birthday Blaire is written on top in green frosting, but both Ys are more on the side of the cake then on top of it. But it's the first time I can remember that anyone actually *baked* me a cake.

When Marcus and I were little, Mom would buy a six pack of cupcakes at the supermarket on her way home from work and stick a candle in each one. Once I was about ten, she decided we were too old for birthday cake. Or, at least that's what she said. I always suspected she just forgot to stop at the store.

"This is the most awesome cake I've ever had," I tell them truthfully.

"What are you guys doing for dinner?" Aimee asks.

I look at the chapters I still have to review before tomorrow. "That sorry ass birthday cake, I'm pretty sure."

"No way," Dee says, grabbing my hand and dragging me toward the door. "It's your birthday."

I pry my hand away. "I don't think Professor Canton gives a shit. I'm barely squeaking by with a C in his class. I need to kick this final's ass or they're going to pull my scholarship money next year."

Aimee splits a glance between us. "Listen, if you need to study, why don't we take Nate out to The Bowl so he can see what we do for fun around here and you can get some work done. We'll have a drink in your honor."

I look at Nate, pleading with my eyes for him to say yes.

"Yeah, okay," he says, giving me a nod. "So what's this Bowl?"

"It's an all-ages club in Oakland with this outdoor stage," Aimee says as Dee and Mike file into the hall. Nate steps through the door and gives me a wave as Aimee keeps talking. "They get these great indie bands all year and..." The door closes and I hear her voice fade down the hall.

I dive into my book and have gotten through enough of it that I feel like I might actually pass my final when they all spill back into the room three hours later, laughing and holding each other up. We spend the next hour eating cake—which despite its pathetic appearance, tastes amazing—and shooting the shit.

Finally, when they've started sobering up, Mike stands from where he's sitting on my desk. "Got an eight o'clock final," he says as he tugs Dee out of my desk chair by the hand. "The prof locks the door at the start of the exam and if you're like one second late, you're shit out of luck."

"'Night," I say as they disappear through the door, leaving it open behind them.

Nate scoots off the bed next to me and pulls me up. "You got a toothbrush I can borrow, babe? Left mine in the car."

I give him my extra toothbrush and let him into the guy's bathroom on my way to the girls. I pee and brush my teeth and when I get back to the room, Nate is stripped down to his boxers, already in my bed.

"Come give papa some sugar," he says, lifting the covers for me.

I climb in next to him and lay with my back to him. Nate spoons me and sucks my earlobe as Aimee comes back from the bathroom in her Hello Kitty tank top and pink flannel PJ pants.

This is a little awkward. Neither of us has had a boyfriend sleep over in our room before. She's been with hers, a cute guy named Erik, for almost three years, since the start of junior year in high school, but he goes to school back east. I met him once when he helped her move in, but he went home with Aimee's parents that night.

"You guys good?" she asks with a hand on the light switch near the door.

"Yeah," I say.

She flips off the light on her way to her bed. "'Night," she says as she climbs in, like this isn't weird at all, so I decide not to worry.

Nate spoons tighter against my back and wraps his arms around me, kissing my neck. And the room goes quiet.

A little while later, Aimee starts to mutter under her breath. She always does that as she's falling asleep and just before she wakes up. And then I feel Nate pressing his hard-on against my ass. He slides a hand under the front of my panties and glides his fingers between my legs.

"Nate, we're not alone," I whisper.

"She's asleep." He dips his middle finger inside me. "I want to give you that birthday present I promised you."

"She might wake up."

"God, baby, please," he begs. "It's been *so* long and I want you so much. You're all I can think about." His fingers pick up pace as he talks, and his breathing is getting heavier on my neck. He kisses my neck and shoulder as he inches my underwear over my hips. Even without my help, he manages to get them down to my thighs "I love you so much," he whispers. "*Please*, baby. I need you."

I feel him behind me wrestling with his boxers, then he rolls on top of me. I turn my face to the side so I don't suffocate when his weight lowers onto my back. He lifts my ass a little as he wedges between my legs. "We'll be quiet," he whispers into my hair. "She'll never know."

Nate starts slow, easing himself into me from behind, but it's only a minute later that the slap of skin as he pounds me is loud enough I'm sure Dee can hear it across the hall. I bury my face in the pillow until he comes with a low rumbling groan deep in his chest.

He collapses on top of me. "Fuck, I missed you."

"I missed you too," I whisper.

"I fucking love you, baby."

I lay here feeling his warmth against my back, feeling him breathe slow and deep, and realize if I stop comparing Nate to Caiden, I could be happy. He says he loves me. I've *always* loved him. This could turn into something if I'd let it.

If I can let go of the hope of Caiden.

After several minutes, when I feel his dick wither enough that it falls out of me on its own, I realize he's asleep. I squirm out from under him and go to the bathroom to clean up.

I went to the student health center when I got to campus last fall and went on the pill, but I've since decided I like condoms better. All the mess ends up in a tidy little package that way. I get myself put together and tiptoe back into the room.

Nate is sprawled face down and naked across my whole bed. As I crawl over him, I realize this is the first time I've had to actually *sleep* with him. He usually leaves when he's done. I wedge myself between him and the wall and steal all the covers.

The studying paid off. I'm pretty sure I killed my last final. If I scored at least a ninety, that would bring me up to a B in Dr. Canton's class to go with all my other As I nailed this semester. It's a huge improvement over last semester and should keep me my scholarship.

Aimee, Dee, Mike, and Nate all decide to go out to The Bowl again tonight, and this time I join them. It's loud and packed, everyone out for one last good time before heading home for the summer. We dance as a group and in pairs, everyone rotating so Aimee doesn't feel like a fifth wheel. Mike is a junior and the only one of us who's twenty-one. He buys us all a few rounds of beer on the sly. We're laughing and sweating and dancing until The Bowl closes down at two and throws everyone out.

"I think I'll hang out with Dee and Mike for a while," Aimee says with a wink at me when we get back to the dorm. My cheeks heat when I realize by the look she gives me that she heard us last night. "Maybe a half hour or so? Does that sound okay?"

My smile is really more of a cringe. "Yeah, okay. Thanks."

Nate closes the door to our room and throws me onto the bed. "You hear that, woman? We've got a half hour to get nasty."

I sit up on the edge of the bed and give him an incredulous look. "Did you just call me 'woman'?"

He yanks his T-shirt over his head and thumps on his chest with his fists like a gorilla, except I think he thinks he's being a caveman. "Me man. You woman."

I shrug. "Guess I shouldn't complain. It's a big improvement over 'baby girl.'"

He stops pounding on himself and looks stricken. "What's wrong with baby girl?"

I think about Caiden, how I really was too much of a baby to be with him. "Just not how I like to think of myself."

He juts his chin and gives a nod. "Okay, I'll just call you 'woman' from now on." He undoes his jeans as he saunters over. He wedges between my knees and pulls out his stiffy. "Dick, meet woman. Woman, this is Dick." He grins dimples down at me as he braces his knees against the mattress between my legs and presses his pelvis forward, so his hard-on is right in my face. He laces his fingers around the nape of my neck and his eyes flash. There's no question what he's asking for.

I've never gone down on anyone but Caiden.

I try to block the thought as I take Nate's dick in my hand and lean forward. When I part my lips over the head, he grasps the back of my neck and plunges himself deeper into my mouth.

"Fuck, yeah, woman," he groans. "You've got lips that were made for this."

I suck on him and he pumps into me, gagging me more than once. I expect a heads up or something when he's getting close, but instead, he grasps me tighter by the hair and thrusts hard into the back of my mouth, unloading down my throat.

He growls as he comes, then his hands loosen in my hair. "I love you, baby."

I swallow and take my mouth off him. "I love you too."

I go to the bathroom a few minutes later and get ready for bed. On the way back, I knock on Dee's door to tell Aimee it's okay to come back in. But when Dee opens the door, Mike is gone and, where Aimee had been laughing when we got home, now she's bawling into Dee's pillow.

"What happened?" I ask.

"Erik sent a sort of weird text," Dee says with a cringe. "Said he'd been thinking about some things and he and Aimee needed to talk when he gets home next week. She thinks he's breaking up with her."

"Shit." I go over to her and sit on the edge of the bed. "Hey, Aim? Why don't you come back to the room? We can pop some popcorn and watch a movie or something."

She lifts her face out of the pillow. "I really don't want to seem this needy in front of your boyfriend," she says, sitting up.

"He's not that sensitive to stuff like this. If the movie's got car chases and explosions, he probably won't even notice you're crying."

She smiles a little. "You're sure?"

"Yeah. Come on."

She gives Dee a hug and I guide her back across the hall. When we open the door, Nate's sprawled shirtless on my bed. At least he had the good sense to fasten his pants.

I pick up his T-shirt, where it still lays crumpled on the floor near the door, and toss it at him. "We're going to put in a movie."

"What you got?" he asks, tugging his shirt on and going to Aimee's box of DVDs under the TV in the corner.

"I don't even remember what I brought," she says. "Just pick whatever looks good."

He comes out with one of the X-men movies and Aimee goes to the bathroom to get ready for bed as he queues it up in the player.

"What's going on?" Nate asks while she's gone.

"Her three-year boyfriend is breaking up with her."

He pulls a face, and I think he's getting ready to make some crack about needy chicks or something. He shocks me by saying, "That sucks. She seems like a decent kid."

"Yeah."

I'm a little surprised I care enough to have a lump in the pit of my stomach on her behalf. I was pretty wary about the whole roommate situation when I got to Berkeley last fall. I'm not a big sharer, so Zoey was a perfect friend. She was generally too hung up on her own shit to dig too deeply into mine. Aimee annoyed the living hell out of me most of first semester. She's just way the fuck too peppy. But I've gotten used to her and she's turned out to be a good friend.

When she gets back from the bathroom in her jammies, she flips off the overhead light and we all pile onto my bed, because it has a better view of the TV. Nate props my pillows against the wall and wedges himself in between Aimee and me. He throws an arm around each of us, then leans his forehead into hers. "He's a dick. You can do better."

She smiles a little and lifts a hand to squeeze Nate's, where it rests on her shoulder. "Not sure that's true, but thanks."

He turns and smiles at me, and my heart warms when I see the compassion in his eyes. He really can be a good guy when he wants to be. I should give him more credit.

He gives me a long kiss, then fast forwards through the rest of the previews.

The movie starts and we lean back against the wall and watch. We're barely through the opening credits and I'm already struggling to keep my eyes open. Nate pulls my head to his shoulder and fingers my hair, and it's so soothing that a few minutes into the movie, I feel myself losing the battle. It's been a stressful week. I tuck my legs under me and settle my body heavier against Nate's. He kisses my forehead and continues to stroke my hair.

I decide to close my eyes for just a minute, just a quick power nap. Then I'll be good to go.

I'm aware that the place I am right now—in Caiden's bed, my legs twisted into his and his soft breath in my hair—is just a dream. It's one of those super realistic dreams, though. Probably because, when I really was in this place, it was the happiest I've been in my life. But I'm hovering on that edge between wake and sleep, with just enough awareness to know that it can't be real. Caiden's gone.

I want to stay here, wrapped in Caiden's warm, earthy scent forever. But the sound of someone knocking on the door pushes me off that razor's edge from asleep to awake. I try to open my eyes and tell them to go away, but I'm still asleep enough that neither my eyes nor mouth will work.

The knocking grows louder and picks up in pace. I roll on my back and throw an elbow over my face, trying to hold onto Caiden for just a few more minutes.

The muffled sound of someone groaning cuts through my fantasy.

My eyes snap open and I sit up. All of a sudden, my heart is pounding in my throat.

The room is pitch black, but what I instantly know is the sound's not someone knocking on the door. It's something banging against the wall. The sound of creaking starts keeping time with the banging. There's a moan and the rustling of sheets.

I reach for the flashlight on the shelf next to my bed and click it on, shining it in the direction of the sound.

My roommate is on her back in her bed, her flannel PJ pants dangling from one ankle and my sweaty boyfriend bouncing between her legs.

Nate stops pumping and his eyes flash in the light like a raccoon caught raiding the neighbor's garbage can. He jumps off her, his latex sheathed hard-on glistening in the flashlight with my roommate's cum.

"Well, at least you were safe," I spit.

Nate yanks his boxers up his thighs and puts his dick away, condom and all.

I throw the covers off and bolt for the door, but Nate lunges for me. He gets ahold of my arm and spins me around. "It's not what you think, babe."

"That's seriously what you're going with? Because I'm pretty sure I just saw you riding my roommate like the fucking Energizer Bunny!"

"Oh, God," I hear Aimee whimper. There's a flurry of movement in the fringes of light as she scrambles to get dressed. "Blaire, please. It was just…we…" Her mouth keeps moving but words stop coming. She finally gets her pants up and tied and moves a step closer, into the light. Tears glisten on her cheeks. "You can't tell Erik."

Rage boils up inside me and it's a damn good thing for both of them it's a flashlight in my hand rather than something sharp. "You know what, Aimee? Fuck you."

I turn for the door again, but Nate grabs me and pins my back against it with a hand on each shoulder.

"Babe, please," he says. "Just hear me out."

I yank out of his grip and huff a derisive laugh, then flip the switch next to the door for the overhead light and cross my arms over my chest. "Okay. I'm listening."

He squints in the sudden bright light, his eyes flashing to Aimee and back. "We didn't mean for it to go there. She was just sort of…fucked up, and we started talking during the movie and—"

"And you thought you'd fuck her better?" I cut in. "Is that your version of kissing her booboo?"

"It's my fault," Aimee interjects. "Erik is the only boy I've ever been with. I love him so much, and now he's just…gone. I needed to…feel something I guess."

I cut her a glare. "So you decided to *feel* my boyfriend."

She drops to her bed and buries her face in her hands.

"You know what? You can have him," I say, throwing a hand at Nate. "I'm done with him."

With the words comes an unexpected but overwhelming sense of liberation. The rush is intense. My skin pebbles into goose bumps. My fingers, toes, and lips tingle as if they've been asleep for a very long time and are just coming back to life. Tears suddenly stream in a river down my face.

And the nagging ache that's lived in my right hip for the last year flares into the searing pain I felt that night a year ago.

It takes a second for the reason for my body's intense reaction to click in my head. Aimee just did me a huge favor. I've spent a year in a relationship with a boy who raped me, and it was slowly killing me. Dampening all my senses. Binding my spirit. Crushing my soul.

I go to Aimee and give her a hug. "If you want to finish fucking him, I'm going to leave for a few minutes." I draw back and look at her. "A half hour or so? Does that sound okay?"

"Oh, God," she sobs when she realizes I'm mocking her.

I turn to Nate and kiss him on the mouth. "And when I come back, I want you the fuck out of my life."

I step through the door and take the stairs down to the first floor. I walk out into the cool night, find a bench along the footpath to the lecture halls. I lay on my back, staring up at the stars. They rush down on me in a shower of sparks and make me dizzy, so that even as tears stream into my ears, I'm laughing. The moon hangs low in the sky, a narrow crescent turned on its side like a smile.

I smile back as I soar with the cosmos. Because for the first time in a long time, I feel free.

CHAPTER 24

Caiden

Hannah is laying on the couch, her feet on the armrest and her head in my lap. She's reading an advanced copy of a book she's apparently not enjoying, based on the hint of a cringe that's been brushing over her features off and on for the last half hour.

I channel surf instead of telling her not to waste her time, because it's her job. Her mom hired her as a literary reviewer for one of the fashion magazines she edits after Hannah completed her PhD in December. She also contributes short stories under a pseudonym to several literary magazines. She gets paid peanuts for both, but she loves it. I know her parents send her money every month to cover our expenses. I also know they never come here because they hate that she's shacking up with a child molester. But Hannah and I never talk about it.

I gave up my apartment in East Overton at the first of the year, partly because I couldn't afford to keep it and partly because Hannah hated sleeping there. Only because Hannah begged, her mom has hooked me up with a few freelance editing gigs, but they're sporadic and they don't pay much. I felt like keeping my apartment was an indulgence. It just made sense to consolidate, since we'd basically been living together since August anyway.

"How long have we known each other, Caiden?" she asks absently, her eyes still sweeping left to right across the page of her book.

"I don't know." I stop on *The Big Bang Theory*. "Maybe three years."

"And we've been sleeping together periodically for most of that."

It's not a question, but I nod.

She swings around and sits up next to me, setting her book on the coffee table. "And for the last five months, we've been living together…sharing expenses, chores, our bed."

I set down the remote on the arm of the couch and look at her. "It feels like you're going somewhere with this."

She holds my gaze. "Where is this ultimately headed? Where do you see our relationship in a year?"

"I don't know, Hannah. A lot of shit can happen in a year." My head spins with all the shit that's happened in the *last* year.

"Point conceded. But if you could choose your own path for the next five years, what would it be?"

This is new. Hannah's never asked me to define what we're doing. Which is what's made it so easy to do. Because when I have to think too much about it, I realize how much this isn't what I want. After whatever was happening between Blaire and I, this feels vapid.

But I'm not a good person. Maybe vapid is all I deserve.

"I haven't thought that much about it."

"Marriage? Children? What do you *want*, Caiden?"

I feel the vein in my temple start to pulse as a searing headache forms behind my right eye. "I have no fucking clue, Hannah! My life is a disaster that I'm not sure can be saved. Haven't you figured that out yet?"

She brings her legs up Indian-style on the couch and turns to face me. She takes my hand and hooks her fingers loosely into mine. "I think you're getting hung up because we're talking in abstracts. I'll give you something more concrete. Do you love me, yes or no?"

Fuck. "Hannah, I don't know."

"I'll take that as a no."

"Hannah—"

"If I were to ask you to marry me right now, what would your answer be, yes or no?"

"Jesus." I rub my throbbing eye, wondering why the hell she thinks she'd want to marry me even if I said yes. "I'd have to think about it."

She nods and unpins me from her gaze. "I guess that's the answer, then. If you were ever going to love me, it would have happened by now."

"You can't tell me *you* love *me*," I say as she gains her feet. I've given her absolutely no reason to.

She looks down at me a long moment. "There are parts of you I love, Caiden. You're compassionate and caring; you have a huge heart and an old soul; and when you aren't trying to prove to yourself that you don't deserve love, you give it really well. I guess I'd started thinking that might be enough." She shakes her head and goes to the fridge. "You want anything?"

"No. Thanks." I feel like I've failed as a human being. Again. I've never done anything but disappoint the people who dare to try to love me.

She comes back with an open Heineken and takes a long swallow as she sinks into the cushions next to me. "So, here's how I see it. If you're not ever going to get over her, you have no choice but to go after her."

When I realize what she's saying, my heart starts to pound in my throat.

"Hasn't she turned eighteen already?" she asks.

"Yesterday."

And now I understand why we're having this conversation *today*. Hannah knows why I spent most of yesterday just drunk enough to keep the memories at bay.

"If she'd extended the restraining order," she says, "wouldn't someone have had to notify you?"

I shake my head. "It doesn't matter. It's been a year. She's moved on—started dating someone her own age. If she's managed to make a normal life for herself, it would be supremely selfish for me to show up expecting her to drop everything and come running back to me now that she's legal. I'm still eight years older than her. That hasn't changed."

She takes a long draw off her beer and we both stare mindlessly at the TV for the next several minutes until the end of the show.

She leans across me and takes the remote from the armrest, clicking off the TV. "Do you remember my theory on obstacles?"

It was her obstacle speech that inspired me to go after Blaire in the first place...which ended with Blaire publicly humiliated and me in jail.

"Did she love you?" she asks when I don't answer her obstacle question.

I shrug. She said she did, but teenage emotions are tricky to pin down. "It felt like it," I answer honestly. "At the time."

"What if she still does, and she's sitting home thinking the same thing you are—that you've moved on and you're better off without her." She smiles a little sadly. "Which, by the way, I would have to agree with, but that's just my opinion."

I huff out a laugh, but the moment passes, and as my smile fades, I'm left with an aching need in the pit of my stomach. "She's with someone her own age," I repeat, trying to keep my head on straight.

"So are you." She lifts a hand to my face and brushes her fingers along the beard I've grown since she and I started doing whatever it is we're doing. "Maybe it's time to stop hiding behind it."

My heart thuds in my chest.

What if she's right?

CHAPTER 25

Blaire

When I went back to my room at dawn, Nate was gone. So was Aimee. I have no idea if they finished fucking or just went their separate ways. I showered, then packed as much as would fit in my Mini and left the rest for Aimee to deal with.

Storm clouds roll in as I drive, and by the time I hit the valley, it's pouring—probably the last spring rain before everything dries up and turns brown for the summer. My tires suck, apparently, and I have to slow way down when I start skidding in the puddles. The rain makes what's normally a three hour drive into four.

I bypass my exit on the highway, same as I did at Christmas break, and drive straight to East Overton. But as I pull into Caiden's parking lot, I'm suddenly terrified.

It's been a year. What if he's found someone society deems more appropriate to love? The blonde looked like she was in her twenties. What if he's in a serious relationship? What if he takes one look at me and wonders what the hell he was thinking?

I take a deep breath. Then another. Finally, as the raindrops begin to slow, I step out of my overflowing car and march up the stairs to Caiden's door.

I knock.

No answer. But I can hear a TV inside.

After a minute, I knock again.

The door flies open and an old Hispanic man with a belly so round it sags out from under his dirty T-shirt answers.

"Qué?"

I glance quickly around to be sure I have the right apartment. "Did Caiden Brenner move?"

He shakes his hands at me like windshield wipers. "No Inglés."

I wipe my palms on my skirt and look around again. At the other end of the parking lot are a bunch of guys. Probably the same ones who wanted me to come out and play when I was stalking Caiden before Christmas.

"I'm sorry," I tell the man in the door, then spin and skip down the stairs.

I'm not even halfway to the group when one of them sees me coming. He starts strutting toward me and his hombres follow.

"Pretty white girl be slummin' it? Tired of missionary and come lookin' for a real live bad boy to satisfy you, Peaches?"

I stand my ground. "Do you know what happened to the guy who used to live in that apartment?" I ask, pointing back the way I came.

"The Professor?" He grins, showing me his gold teeth. Yep, same guy. "I might got some information." He starts unbuckling his belt. "What the pretty girl willin' to give me for it?"

"I need to know where he went."

Desperation causes the words to come out a little choked, which only spurs Gold Teeth on. "You ever suck Mexican dick, Peaches?" He grins. "We're spicy. You like it."

He's got his junk half out of his pants when one of his hombres comes up behind him and smacks him upside the head.

"Why you always gotta be a fuckin' asshole, Manuel? Nobody want to see your fuckin' junk." He steps around Manuel and looks at me. "The Professor, he moved some shit outta here around New Years. Otis let us take the rest of the shit he left in there. Ain't none of us seen him or his sweet blonde since then."

"Who would know where he went? Maybe someone in the office? Otis?"

"Ain't no office. Otis runs the place when he ain't fuckin' passed out. He don't know nothin'."

I take a deep breath to settle the acid rising up my throat. I look around the lot for Caiden's car, knowing I'm not going to find it.

I turn back to the guy. "Was the blonde here a lot? Before he moved out?"

He gives a loose, whole body shrug. "None of them been around much since last summer."

"But when he was here, so was her fine ass," Gold Teeth interjects with a shit-eating grin, grabbing his junk, which he's thankfully put away.

My stomach sinks through my shoes. They've been together since last summer. Probably since he got out of jail. "Thanks."

I go back to my car and stare at my phone for about a year before working up the nerve to dial. I throw my phone into the passenger door when the message says Caiden's number has been disconnected.

There's only one thing I can think to do. Out of sheer desperation, I drive to Sierra State. If it means finding Caiden, I'm willing to face Professor Duncan again. I knock on his door, but it's locked and there's no answer.

The next door down the hall is open. The nameplate next to the door says *Dr. Gerald Garret*. I stick my head in and find an older guy, balding with horn-rimmed glasses, sitting behind the desk. It looks like he's falling asleep over some papers he's reading.

"Hi," I say and he jumps and straightens himself in his seat.

"Can I help you?"

I step into the door. "I know Caiden Brenner isn't at this school anymore, but he's moved since he worked here. Do you know if there's someone who might know where I can find him?"

His face twists as if he just ate something rotten. "He's been gone a year. If he's not at the address in his employment record, we wouldn't have had any reason to update it.

So, that's it. He's gone. He's moved on with his life.

"Thank you," I say, already turning for the stairs.

I drop into my car and pull out of the lot as the first tears roll down my face. When the road ahead of me gets so blurry I nearly hit an oncoming car, I pull over to the shoulder. I fold my arms over the steering wheel and rest my forehead on them as sobs hitch up from the deepest part of me. Every muscle clenches as my body vomits out the pain in a river of tears, leaving me raw and bleeding inside.

This is when I know what Nate did for me. I traded this pain for the numb humiliation being with him brought me. A voice slithering through the darkest corners of my mind whispers to me to go back to the numbness. But that's sick, and I've already been sick for too long.

So I pull my head up, scrub my face clean with my sleeve, embrace my mangled life, and drive home.

I'm relieved to find that neither of my parents' or Nate's cars are parked out front when I pull up to the house. I unlock the front door and when I push it open, the first thing I see is Marcus, sprawled on the family room floor with an ice bag on his hand and his other elbow crooked over his eyes.

"What happened?"

He uncovers his face and I see a welt rising on his left cheekbone when he sits up. He bends his knees up and wraps his elbows around them, shaking his head.

I slide onto the floor next to him and poke at his cheek. "Are you okay?"

"No."

I wave a hand in front of his face and look into his pupils. "Are you dizzy? Do you think you have a concussion or something?"

"No. I just have a walking douchebag for a best friend."

Oh, shit. "What happened?"

He scratches the top of his head. "Nate said you broke up with him. When I asked why, he told me to ask you. When I said I was asking *him*, he muttered something about your roommate being hot and it wasn't his fault, so I fucking leveled him."

My heart squeezes into a hard ball and I feel sick. "Thanks, but he's totally not worth it."

He drags himself to his feet, flexing the knuckles of his right hand. He holds his left out to me and I take it. "But you are," he says, pulling me off the floor. "There's a reason I didn't want him anywhere near you. He'll fuck anything that walks."

I only realize my eyes are welling when Marcus tugs me to his chest. It feels so good to be back in his arms. I let things stay bad between us for too long, but I understand why now. I knew Marcus would be the only person who'd look close enough to see that I was dead inside. If I pushed him away, I was safe to self-destruct without anyone trying to stop me.

Seeing how he reacted to what happened with Caiden, I know I can never tell him Nate raped me. He'd think it was his fault, somehow, and he'd never forgive himself for not protecting me. But I need his arms so badly right now.

"It's always been us against the world, Blaire," he says. "That hasn't changed. The only difference is that that cocksucker is now part of 'the world' instead of 'us.'"

"When did our lives get so fucked up?" I ask into his T-shirt.

"When Dad looked at Mom with that lusty spark in his eye."

I hear the smile in his voice and laugh through my tears, blowing snot out my nose onto his T-shirt. "Nothing good could ever come of that."

CHAPTER 26

Caiden

She arrives at Tino's alone tonight and sits with the same group of poets at a table up front. I watch from the barstool in the darkest corner, but instead of scotch, I'm drinking Coke.

There are five poets who read, and Blaire listens intently to each one. When Gloria is introduced, she squeezes Blaire's shoulder on her way to the stage. She finishes and after her scores post, the room goes quiet and the MC, Craig, looks at Blaire like he's going to eat her alive when he says, "We've got a special performance tonight, a returning house favorite, racking up sixty-three wins over a two-year period before she left us for bigger and better things. Please welcome back to the Tino's stage, our very own, Blaire Leon!"

She makes her way slowly up the stairs and Craig wraps her whole body in a long, tight hug. He whispers something in her ear and her eyes are wide with...shock? disgust? when she pulls away from him. She watches him leave the stage and takes a minute to collect herself before she steps up to the mic.

When the bright spotlight hits her face, my heart lurches.

She looks drawn, purple circles in the hollows of lifeless amber eyes; the glow in that fair complexion gone, as if life has beaten her down and robbed her of her contagious spirit.

She stands in front of the mic collecting herself for longer than usual, and when a tear courses down her face, she makes no move to wipe it away.

She takes one last breath, then lifts her head and starts.

"Have you ever thought: What's it all for? I don't mean after a particularly bad day, when your whole life is sliding into a steaming shithole. I mean, have you ever sat down and *really* contemplated the point of life?"

Even with the tear, her voice starts light. A little whimsical.

"Is the point of life success? But how do you know when you've achieved *enough* success? How do you quantify it? Measure it? Is it how much you know? IQ points? The number of degrees you hold? Or does a sharp mind only make you more capable of justifying even your worst decisions? Maybe success is measured in the number of friends you have on speed dial? But then how do you determine which of your collection would gladly throw you under the bus when it's in their own best interests?" She shakes her head. "So if it's not knowledge or friends, maybe success is money? But if someone else has more than you, how can you know if you've hit the benchmark? Is it truly the guy who dies with the most toys who wins?"

Her tone becomes harder and takes on more of a bitter edge as she progresses. I start focusing on every word, trying to ferret out what she's telling me about her life in between the lines.

"Is the point of life happiness? Are rats on a treadmill happy? If they could speak, they'd probably tell you they're not *un*happy," she says with a lift of her hand. "They get on that fucking wheel of their own volition every. Single. Day. And they run themselves into the ground. So, what is happiness? How do you know when you're happy? Is happiness just the absence of sadness? Is the point of life just not to be sad?"

My heart hammers so hard in my chest I can see each beat ripple the fluid in the glass I'm gripping so tightly it's in danger of shattering. If anyone deserves to be happy, it's Blaire. But she's quite obviously profoundly sad.

"Or maybe the Beatles really were tapped into the universal consciousness and all we need is love. Maybe *love* is the golden ring on the carousel of life. Could it be that we're intended to spend our days perusing a transient and ethereal emotion? Something so fleeting that, when you grip it too tightly, it slips through your fingers and vanishes like smoke on a breeze? Something that repeatedly leaves your heart ripped open and bleeding out any hope that it even exists?"

The peal of anguish lacing her words rips *my* heart open. She's not been hurt by love. She's been destroyed by it. Acid rolls up my throat, knowing I played a part in that.

"Even if the point of life is just not dying, we all fail there eventually too."

She pulls the mic from the stand and walks to the side of the stage. "From where I stand, life looks something like this: We get up. We get up. We get up," she says, raising the hand not holding the mic higher with each "up."

She drops her hand. "We fall down."

She moves to the other side of the stage. "We get up. We get up. We get up," she says, repeating the process.

"We fall down."

She comes back to the middle of the stage and sits at the edge with her legs dangling. "Sometimes we fall on our own." She holds a hand palm out to the audience, then thrusts it forward. "Sometimes we're pushed."

Who pushed you, Blaire? Was it me?

"So, is that the point? Because, honestly, it seems the most likely scenario. Life is just some sort of cosmic joke. No matter how hard we strive for happiness, knowledge, love, success, no matter how close we get to grabbing that golden ring, or how sure we are that we get the point of the whole thing, at some point the universe is going to shove us down just to prove us wrong."

I didn't think she saw me, but as she gains her feet, her gaze locks on mine, and I know I'm right. I did this to her.

"There is no fucking carousel ring." She gives her head a bitter shake. "Hell, there's not even a carousel. The joy you felt while you were riding—the certainty that you'd weathered the shit storm of life and the wind in your hair was your reward—it was all just a fucking illusion."

She turns and walks back to the mic stand in the middle of the stage, snapping it back into the bracket.

"The point of life is that it's pointless."

There's a minute of dead silence as she spins for the stairs, and then the group at her table in the front stands and starts to clap. Within a few seconds, the whole room is standing.

But Blaire doesn't stop for the hugs or high fives she's being offered. She doesn't even seem to notice there are other people in the room. She comes directly to where I'm now standing, next to my barstool, and stops in front of me.

The scores post, but I don't hear a word Craig is saying. All I know is Blaire's desperate gaze.

"You had a beard last time I saw you."

At her statement, my stomach plummets into my shoes. I lift a hand to my freshly shaven face. I only had that beard while I was with Hannah. And I was *always* with Hannah. She was right, I was hiding behind her like a shield. I thought that's what I needed to do. Not for my own safety. For everyone else's. For Blaire's. I needed to keep her safe from *me*.

I take her elbow and usher her to the door. When we hit the sidewalk, she pulls her arm out of my grasp and keeps going. I follow, because, let's face it, I'm helpless to do anything else. I'd follow her into the pits of hell if I could have her there.

"Are you still together?" she asks without looking at me.

"No."

Hannah spent this morning trying to convince me to stay at her place until I could find an apartment I could afford, but I could feel myself already questioning my resolve. It would be too easy to slip back into the same pattern and just hide behind her the rest of my life. So I checked into a seedy pay-by-the-month hotel this afternoon and told her I'd be back for the few things in her apartment that are mine when I had somewhere to put them. I shaved, slept for a few hours, then got in my car and drove to Tino's.

About half a block up, I see her car. She reaches into her pocket and the lights flash as she clicks the lock. She lowers herself into the driver's seat, but when I try the passenger door, it's still locked. She slams her door and cranks the stereo. Arctic Monkeys shake her windows.

It's been a long time since I've let myself listen to that song.

When she makes no move to unlock the door, I pace to the car parked ahead of hers and lean against the trunk.

Inside her car, "Do I Wanna Know?" plays on repeat, asking if this feeling flows both ways. I pray to God her answer is yes.

Her forehead is propped against the wheel. She doesn't move.

For the next half hour.

So I wait. If she drives away, I'll let her, but only because I know she understands what she's leaving behind. She's making her choice, and I have no choice but to let her.

Finally, she lifts her head and her eyes find mine. I hold her gaze and try to convey everything I'm feeling with a glance. I want her to feel me to her soul and know everything I am is hers if she wants me.

She opens the door and gets out. I shove off the car and face her.

"Do I want to know?" she asks.

I nod and take a step forward, but her expression is one of a feral animal, cornered and scared.

"*Do I want to fucking know, Caiden?*" she growls through gritted teeth, shoving both hands into my chest and knocking me back a step.

I hold my arms to the side, bearing myself open for whatever she needs to do. "Whatever you want is yours, whether it's just my body, or my heart and soul too. You own me, Blaire. You always have."

She comes at me again, but this time, instead of pushing me, she slams into me, her arms reaching around me and gripping so tightly I feel my ribs pop.

I fold my arms around her and press my face to the crown of her hair. "No more holding back. I'll tell you everything."

"Tell me," she says into my shirt.

I lift her face and look into her eyes, trying to make her feel my words. "I agree with almost everything you said in your poem just now. We all spend our whole fucking lives grabbing at shiny things we think will make us happy—all the ridiculous benchmarks that we or people around us have set to measure our worth. We get so caught up in it that I think we lose sight of the things that matter, and when that happens, life is going to feel pointless. But I don't think it is. That's the part I disagree with." I shake my head and thumb the tears from her cheeks. "All I can tell you for sure is I don't have many answers, but I've got one. There has never been a time through any of this that I stopped loving you. *You* are what matters. When I lose sight of you, life *is* pointless. With you here, in my arms—" I lean forward and press my lips to her forehead. "—not so much."

She breathes a shaky breath. "Tell me again. That last part."

I lift her and crush her body to mine. Nothing has ever felt more right. "I love you, Blaire, with everything that I am. As long as you want me, I'm not going anywhere."

Her ankles lock around my hips and she hikes herself higher up my body with her hands around my neck. "I thought I lost you."

"What do you want, Blaire? Tell me what you want from me."

"Take me home," she says, and from the look in her eye, I know she doesn't mean to her parents' house.

I take the keys from her hand and load her into the passenger seat of her Mini. I duck into the driver's seat and pull onto the road. She reaches for my hand on the stick shift and weaves her fingers between mine, then leans her head against my shoulder.

We pull into my cheap no-tell motel fifteen minutes later. I scan my key and guide Blaire through the door into the cramped, musty room. She kicks off her shoes and climbs under the covers in all her clothes. I toe off my Vans and go to the other side, sliding in next to her and wrapping my body around hers.

She falls asleep quickly, exhausted, no doubt. She looks so beaten down. But her body twitches, still wound too tightly to relax, even in sleep. I hold her and send her any shred of peace I can find within myself. I breathe her in and live in this place, where I never thought I'd be again. Eventually, I drift off and dream of being right where I am.

I wake to pale morning light and a warm body draped over mine. When I open my eyes, Blaire is on top of me. Naked.

She smiles down at me and traces the lines of my mouth with the tip of her forefinger, making me smile in return. She pushes herself up so she's straddling my hips and starts on the button of my jeans.

I strip my T-shirt off as she works my fly, then let her drag my jeans down my legs.

On the way back up, she slows to give my raging hard-on a tongue bath. When she teabags my balls, they pull tight and I groan. She licks from base to tip again, but just as she opens her lips to sheath my cock with that hot, wet mouth, I reach for her arms and drag her up my body. "I want to be inside you when I come."

I reach for my wallet on the nightstand, but she grasps my hand and lays it on her breast. She lift her hips and positions the head of my erection at her opening. "I'm on the pill."

She rolls her hips, taking me inside, and Christ, she's tight. I feel the full measure of my aching cock sinking through her slick folds until I'm seated to the root inside her. She starts to rock her pelvis on mine and I grasp her hips and move to her rhythm.

I trail my fingers over those perfect C cups, down flat, tight abs, to the center of her world. I work her clit and she starts to moan, a feral sound from deep inside her. Her hand cups her breast and she rolls the nipple under her thumb. The fingers of her other hand follow mine between her legs. She mimics the movement of my thumb with her fingers. After a minute, I slip my hand out and watch as she continues to work her clit.

I grasp her hips and pump harder, thrusting as deeply into her as I can, desperate to moor myself so far inside her that no one can dig me out. It's not long before her inner muscles clamp hard around my cock as she screams out her release. I come hard just behind her, because watching her get herself off with me inside her is one of the hottest fucking things I've ever seen.

She lowers herself onto my chest. "I wanted to know how you do it. I've never been able to come on my own."

"I find that hard to believe." Her body is so receptive. She just rides the waves of desire with no inhibitions.

"I've never really been close except with you." Her tongue laps a ring around my nipple before she sucks it. "I can't seem to really let go if we're not together…like I need your energy or our connection or something for my body to work right."

I wrap my arms around her. "We were made for this."

She rocks her hips against mine and grins down at me. "Then I think we should do it again."

I smile and roll her onto her back. She spreads wide and I start to move inside her, my cock already pulsing with the influx of blood as it hardens again.

She smiles up at me and something wicked flashes in her eyes. "I think we should send Detective Diaz a sex tape. She seemed to enjoy the one Craig made."

"Craig?"

"He told me tonight that he followed us. He wanted to go out after the slam tonight and said I wouldn't regret it. Said he could make me come like you did."

My blood pressure rises twenty points, and I literally see red as it pumps hard through my head. But I'm not going to let him ruin what we've got going right this second. I kiss her then start pumping inside her. "You're killing the mood, love."

She grins up at me. "Did you just call me 'love.'"

"I did."

She pulls my mouth to hers and kisses me to my soul. "I like that," she says when she finally releases me.

I love her slowly, living in her body. And when she never asks to go home, I never take her.

EPILOGUE

Blaire

The Complete Works of William Blake is open on the arm of the sofa in front of me. I'm on my stomach, propped on my elbows, reading. Caiden's leaning back against the other armrest. His knees are bent and his feet press against my outer thighs. The tops of my feet rest in the creases of his hips. His laptop lays on the back of my calves as he works.

"You weren't joking about Blake being warped," I say, then clear my throat and start reading *A Poison Tree* aloud.

"I was angry with my friend:
I told my wrath, my wrath did end.
I was angry with my foe:
I told it not, my wrath did grow.

"And I watered it in fears,
Night and morning with my tears:
And I sunned it with smiles,

And with soft deceitful wiles.

"And it grew both day and night,
Till it bore an apple bright.
And my foe beheld it shine,
And he knew that it was mine.

"And into my garden stole.
When the night had veiled the pole;
In the morning glad I see;
My foe outstretched beneath the tree."

I look over my shoulder at Caiden. "I thought the last stanza would be some big message about how holding a grudge will destroy you, not about how sweet revenge is."

"Blake wasn't all that into ethical grandstanding. He would have hated all those after-school specials and Hallmark movies with the big moral messages."

"Yeah, but..." I look back at the book. "That's a little over the top, isn't it. I mean, I get that this guy did something to piss him off, but he's saying he basically obsessed over his wrath until he finally killed the guy."

"What makes it even more interesting is that there's a consensus in some literary circles that Blake's apple symbolizes one of his own creative works that one of his contemporaries stole and passed off as their own." He sets his laptop aside and starts massaging my feet. "The fact, as you so deftly pointed out, that there's no final stanza that suggests any remorse for the vengeance would suggest Blake was hoping for an unhappy end to his plagiarist."

I drop my forehead onto the book. "God, that feels good."

He massages deeper. "Chris and Taryn are coming to graduation tomorrow. Chris has some big gift for you that he's keeping secret even from me."

"Seriously?"

We've spent some time with Caiden's brother and his fiancée. I really like them both. But I don't feel like I know them well enough for them to be giving me a gift.

"Are your parents coming?" he asks.

I nod against the book. "And Marcus."

His fingers stall on my feet for a second before he goes back to working his magic. And I know why.

He's never met Marcus.

Caiden moved to Berkeley with me when I came back to school sophomore year. We found our tiny studio apartment over a bar in a not-too-scary neighborhood in Oakland. He had some editing jobs and got a paid internship at a small non-profit in San Francisco, which turned into a full-time archivist position in their Knowledge Services department last year. I sold the Mini and busted my ass to keep my scholarships. I started getting invitations to poetry slams with prize money attached last year, and the more of those I've won, the more invitations I've gotten. We're getting by. Just barely.

But Marcus has never come to see us in Oakland, and the few times we've gone home to visit, he makes a point not to be around, even though he moved home last year after he graduated UCLA. He's coaching the girls' water polo team at Oak Crest High while he's trying to figure out what to do with his Exercise Science degree. In his heart, I think Marcus understands I've always loved Caiden, but he's never gotten past what happened between us when I was only seventeen.

They say time heals all wounds. I hope they're right.

I feel all the tension in my body leech out as Caiden massages. He has that power over me. Just his touch can bring me down from the edge of crazy. His presence, his love, is the only reason I've made it through the last three years at Berkeley with my sanity intact.

He rubs and I melt into the cushions, forgetting all about William Blake. But when his tongue finds my feet and makes totally unrelated parts of me wet, I turn over and watch him suck my toes.

Something on my foot catches the light and flashes. When I look closer, I realize he's slipped a ring onto my toe.

A emerald ring. My birthstone. The emerald is a small and rectangular with tiny diamonds set around the edges.

I wiggle my toes and it shimmers in the sunlight. "My birthday was yesterday. Don't you remember? You took me out for my first legal drink, then brought me home and took advantage of my drunken ass."

He grins. "Oh I remember. All except the part about taking advantage of you. I'm pretty sure *I* was the one being ravaged all night."

I slip the ring off my toe and crawl up Caiden's body, laying across his chest and holding the ring up. "You already gave me a birthday present."

"Then it's a damn good thing this isn't a birthday present." He takes the ring from my hand. "Do you remember what I told you in the street the night I took you home with me and never brought you back?"

"You told me a lot of things," I say, confused.

He rolls the ring in between his finger and thumb. "I said life isn't pointless if you don't lose sight of the things that really matter."

My heart begins to pound when I start to follow what's happening here. "You also said I owned you."

He smiles, slow and sexy. "You do. Every fucking inch of me." He lifts me gently by the hips and slides out from under me, then lowers himself to a knee on the carpet.

I sit up and just stare, unable to form a coherent thought.

"I always believed when I met The One, something about her would speak to me in a way no one else ever had. Ever since that first night in the library at Sierra four and a half years ago, when you were standing there asking about Byron in that baggy sweater and jeans, somewhere in my DNA, I knew it was you. Your spirit speaks to mine. Your soul feeds mine. You unlock all the best parts of me and I'm more when I'm with you. *You* are the thing that gives my life meaning. You keep me from being pointless. If I do any of those things for you"—he holds up the ring—"then marry me, Blaire."

I crack up.

Laughter comes so hard that I double over and can't even speak for several minutes. When I finally pull my shit together, I wipe the moisture from my eyes and I look at Caiden. He lifts his eyebrows in a question.

I hold out my hand and he slides the ring onto my ring finger. "You had me a little worried. I wasn't sure that was a yes."

"It's just, I can't think of a bigger 'fuck you' to the world, you know? They yank us apart and send you to jail for loving me, and now..." I hold up the ring and like how it looks on my hand. "I think we should invite Professor Duncan and his high horse to the wedding."

Caiden's brow creases. "He did the right thing, Blaire. I was a faculty member and you were underage."

I shake my head, hating that I even brought this up to ruin our moment. But I can't help it. I've carried all this resentment and anger for so long. "Firing you was the right thing. Maybe even withholding your degree, though I think that part was really just him having a hissy fit. But he never once asked how *I* felt. He never asked me if *I* wanted to report you to the police. He just assumed I was a naïve little girl who'd been played by a person in a position of authority. He projected all his shit all over me."

Tears begin to stream down my face as the real root of all my anger burns to the surface. Suddenly his face is all I can see, and it's not Professor Duncan.

Caiden tries to hold me and I shove him back. "He decided what you were doing to me was rape, but where the fuck was he three weeks later? No one fucking saved me from Nate! He raped me and I..." I drop my head when a sob hitches up my throat, choking off my words. "I kept going back," I say weakly. "Every time he touched me, it killed another piece of my soul. And I let him. Over and over and over."

I see the animal in Nate's face as he pins me down. I see the possessive look in his eye and I know he hears me when I say no. I feel him, grasping tighter, pounding harder when I try to push him back.

I feel the toxic swamp mud oozing through my veins again. I feel poison, like Blake's apple.

This time, when Caiden pulls me off the sofa and into his arms, I let him.

"I'm so sorry." He crushes me to his chest. "Christ, Blaire, I knew something had happened to you. You weren't the same after..." He presses his face harder into my hair as he shakes his head. "But I just assumed it was me...what happened with us. I didn't know. I'm so sorry."

I manage to gradually pull myself together and wrestle out of Caiden's arms, feeling suddenly stupid. "It doesn't matter. It was a long time ago."

He lets me go, but his eyes stay on mine. "It *does* matter. Blaire, you need to get help…talk to someone who knows about this shit…someone who can help you figure out ways of dealing with it."

I shake my head. "I don't want to talk about it."

He slides onto the sofa next to me and lifts my face so I'm looking into those storming blue eyes. "I think you need to. Jesus, Blaire. You've been carrying this around for so long. It's eating you alive."

I bolt off the sofa when my stomach suddenly turns into a volcano. I make it as far as the tile floor of the bathroom before its acid contents erupt out of me. I collapse onto my hands and knees and wait the waves of nausea out. It's several minutes later that my puking turns to dry heaves, then finally trails off.

It feels like my body's trying to puke out my entire year with Nate. Every touch was poison and I feel it burning my insides on its way out.

When I become aware of my surroundings again, I realize Caiden's on the floor with me, holding my hair back. I sink into his lap and he pulls me close, not even caring that I'm covered with puke. "I love you, Blaire. We're going to get through this. Let me help you."

My whole body seizes and I curl into a ball.

Let me help you.

That shouldn't sound terrifying. But it does.

I've never let myself need anyone. I learned to take care of myself when I was young, and then I took care of Marcus too. But maybe Caiden is right. Maybe the point of life is not to get so lost in the bullshit that you lose sight of what matters.

Caiden matters. *We* matter.

I don't have to be alone anymore. I can tear down my walls and let someone help me. I can let *Caiden* help me, because there's no one I trust more.

I sink deeper into him, right there on the steaming, puke-covered floor, and tell him everything. I open up my mouth and my greasy black soul spills all over him.

"I let myself believe he didn't hear me say no. I let him…" I cringe and trail off. "Every time we were together I felt him rape me all over again, so I just shut down and stopped feeling anything. I turned it all off and just pretended not to exist."

He doesn't flinch or pull away when I give him the details—of the rape and everything after. By the time I'm done, the apartment's dark, but Caiden is still here, holding me. His grip on me is as tight as it started, as if he understands that my greatest fear is him letting go.

"I've got you, love," he whispers in my ear, rocking me slowly in his arms.

Love. He calls me love, like that's what I am to him. Maybe that's all I need to be.

All you need is love.

Fuck. What if The Beatles were right this whole time? Maybe love isn't as transient and ethereal as I thought. Maybe it's the most real thing there is.

He thumbs the ring on my finger. "We've still got some things to figure out, Blaire. I get that. But that's the journey I want to take with you all the way to the 'the grow old and die' scene at the end of Act Five."

I blink at his reference to my graduation speech. He wasn't there. He was in jail.

He smiles at my confusion. "I found your speech when I searched for your poetry on YouTube after I got out of jail."

"You cyberstalked me?" I ask with a lift of my eyebrows. But I can't contain the smile, knowing even when we were apart, he was thinking of me.

He trails a fingertip down my nose. "I was in purgatory the year we were apart. Seeing your face, listening to what came out of that beautiful mind of yours, it was the only thing that saved me."

"Parts of my mind aren't that beautiful." I cringe. "There are dark parts and scary parts and more than a few crazy parts."

"I think it's your dark, scary, and crazy parts that speak to mine." He pulls me close. "Nothing in there could ever scare me away."

I mold myself to his body. "Remember you said that."

I've never believed in "two halves of a whole," or destiny or any of that. I've surrounded myself with people who made it easy for me to be an island. I've chosen to be alone in this life. Until Caiden. Now I know that no one is ever truly alone. That knowledge prickles my skin into goose bumps and steals my breath as the truth sinks into my bones. The connections are there, some stronger than others. The strongest are capable of breaking through any wall we put up.

Caiden was through my walls before I even knew I had them. I don't know if that's destiny, but it's big. And it's real.

Scarily real.

I pull myself out of Caiden's arms and move to the window. The stars are hard to see through the city lights, but they're there. "Does this scare you?"

He comes up behind me and lays his hands gently on my hips. "What scares the living shit out of me is the thought of a life without you in it."

In the black velvet sky above, the moon smiles on me the same way she did the night exactly three years ago when I freed my soul from my self-imposed prison. I smile back knowing that, because of Caiden, I'll never need walls again. And I'll never be alone.

HOW TO HEAL

A poem by Blaire Leon

I can hardly remember when
His touch felt like love on my skin.
Before he forced his way in.
Now every touch feels like a sin.

Distrust has become my law.
Fear rakes my insides raw.
The only chance of survival: Die.
Wave the part of my soul that sang goodbye.

Iron bolt the doors to my heart,
And never again let it start
To remember the part
Where my friend became the monster in the dark.

How many secrets can you keep?
Can you lock away deep?
What will it take to unlock the pain?
Things I can't even begin to explain

Or to understand.
Will it be another hand?
One who loves without command?
A man who knows my heart firsthand?

A voice of unconditional love
That will finally help me rise above
The landmines in my soul;
The scars in my heart that control

The way I cry and love and hate.
The reason for my self-abate
Dies when I dare to open a new slate.
For the way I live and die and create

A place in my spirit that can love again
And trust that he'll not revive the pain.
This is how my soul begins to heal;
By believing in him and keeping it real.

ACKNOWLEDGEMENTS

Heartfelt thanks go first to every single one of you who picked this book up and gave it a try. I truly appreciate you spending your valuable time with Blaire and Caiden. That includes the many bloggers and authors who helped spread the word. Thank you from the bottom of my heart.

This book would not have happened without the encouragement of my dear friend Katy Evans, cheerleader extraordinaire. Thank you, my lovely. And thanks also to the ladies at New Leaf Literary who brought this story to life: Suzie Townsend for all her tireless work on my behalf, and Danielle Barthel for fixing all my many booboos. Thanks to Danielle Sanchez and K.P. Simmon at Inkslinger for all your encouragement and endless hours of support. And, always, thank you to my family for…everything. I love you.

Music is my muse, and I try to give credit to the artists who inspire my work. The influence of a single song caused all the passion that is Caiden and Blaire's story to pour out of me in a matter of days. You'll find that song referenced in the text, but I have to thank Alex Turner of Arctic Monkeys for writing "Do I Wanna Know."

ABOUT THE AUTHOR

Mia Storm is a hopeless romantic who is always searching for her happy ending. Sometimes she's forced to make one up. When that happens, she's thrilled to be able to share those stories with her readers. She lives in California and spends much of her time in the sun with a book in one hand and a mug of black coffee in the other, or hiking the trails in Yosemite. Connect with her online at MiaStormAuthor.blogspot.com, on Twitter at @MiaStormAuthor, and on Facebook at www.facebook.com/MiaStormAuthor.